"Wa... Your Assist... Touched Hi... ...ember Anythin... ...ut My Job."

"Exemplary. You've been far more than my assistant. My right-hand woman is a better description."

She looked pleased. "I guess that's a good thing, since we're getting married."

"Absolutely." Jake swallowed. How would she react when her memory returned and she realized they had never been romantically involved? She wasn't in love with him. Still, that kiss had been surprisingly spicy. In fact, he couldn't remember experiencing anything like it in his fairly substantial kissing experience.

Maybe it was the element of the forbidden. He'd never considered kissing his assistant and it still felt…wrong. Probably because it was wrong of him to let her think they'd been a couple. But once a ring was on her finger, they really would be engaged and everything would be on the up and up.

At least until her memory came back.

Dear Reader,

I've always been attracted to amnesia stories. In fact, the first book I ever wrote—which will never see the harsh light of day!— featured a hero with amnesia. I've written about twenty books since that first brave attempt, but I've always wanted to return to the theme of amnesia and explore it in a new story. There's something so fascinating about someone waking up and having to interact with the world around them without the familiar filter of experience and memory that governs so much of what we do.

In this story, Andi's amnesia allows the characters to step out of their accustomed roles, as monarch/boss and loyal admin, and see each other with fresh eyes. On the other hand, Andi's memory loss gives her no choice but to trust Jake and what he tells her about their relationship, so things get very complicated when her memory returns and she realizes he's taken liberties with the truth.

I hope you enjoy Jake and Andi's romantic (mis)adventures!

Jen

JENNIFER LEWIS

AT HIS MAJESTY'S CONVENIENCE

Recycling programs
for this product may
not exist in your area.

ISBN-13: 978-0-373-73106-0

AT HIS MAJESTY'S CONVENIENCE

www.Harlequin.com

Printed in U.S.A.

Books by Jennifer Lewis

Desire

The Boss's Demand #1812
Seduced for the Inheritance #1830
Black Sheep Billionaire #1847
Prince of Midtown #1891
*Millionaire's Secret Seduction #1925
*In the Argentine's Bed #1931
*The Heir's Scandalous Affair #1938
The Maverick's Virgin Mistress #1977
The Desert Prince #1993
Bachelor's Bought Bride #2012
†The Prince's Pregnant Bride #2082
†At His Majesty's Convenience #2093

*The Hardcastle Progeny
†Royal Rebels

JENNIFER LEWIS

has been dreaming up stories for as long as she can remember and is thrilled to be able to share them with readers. She has lived on both sides of the Atlantic and worked in media and the arts before she grew bold enough to put pen to paper. Happily settled in England with her family, she would love to hear from readers at jen@jenlewis.com. Visit her website at www.jenlewis.com.

Dedication:

For Lulu, a gracious lady and a powerful communicator
who's encouraged me to slow down
and see the big picture.

Acknowledgments:

More thanks to the lovely people who read this book
while I was writing it: Anne, Cynthia, Jerri, Leeanne,
my agent Andrea and my editor Charles.

One

He won't ever forgive you.

Andi Blake watched her boss from the far end of the grand dining room. Dressed in a black dinner jacket, dark hair slicked back, he looked calm, composed and strikingly handsome as usual, while he scanned the printed guest list she'd placed on the sideboard.

Then again, maybe he wouldn't care at all. Nothing rattled Jake Mondragon, which was why he'd transitioned easily from life as a successful Manhattan investor to his new role as king of the mountainous nation of Ruthenia.

Would her departure cause even a single furrow in his majestic brow? Her heart squeezed. Probably not.

Her sweating palms closed around the increasingly crumpled envelope containing her letter of resignation. The letter made it official, not just an idle threat or even a joke.

Do it now, before you lose your nerve.

Her breath caught in her throat. It didn't seem possible to just walk up to him and say, "Jake, I'm leaving." But if she didn't she'd soon be making arrangements for his wedding.

She'd put up with a lot of things in the three years since she'd moved from their lofty office in Manhattan to this rambling Ruthenian palace, but she could not stand to see him marry another woman.

You deserve to have a life. Claim it.

She squared her shoulders and set out across the room, past the long table elegantly set for fifty of his closest friends.

Jake glanced up. Her blood heated—as always—when his dark eyes fixed on hers. "Andi, could you put me next to Maxi Rivenshnell instead of Alia Kronstadt? I sat next to Alia last night at the Hollernsterns and I don't want Maxi to feel neglected."

Andi froze. How could it have become her job to cultivate his romances with these women? Ruthenia's powerful families were jostling and shoving for the chance to see their daughter crowned queen, and no one cared if little Andi from Pittsburgh got trampled in the stampede.

Least of all Jake.

"Why don't I just put you between them?" She tried to keep her tone even. Right now she wanted to throw her carefully typed letter at him. "That way you can kiss up to both of them at once."

Jake glanced up with a raised brow. She never spoke to him like this, so no wonder he looked surprised.

She straightened her shoulders and thrust the letter out at him. "My resignation. I'll be leaving as soon as the party's over."

Jake's gaze didn't waver. "Is this some kind of joke?"

Andi flinched. She'd known he wouldn't believe her.

"I'm totally serious. I'll do my job tonight. I'd never leave you in the lurch in the middle of an event, but I'm leaving first thing tomorrow." She couldn't believe how calm she sounded. "I apologize for not giving two weeks' notice, but I've worked day and night for the last three years in a strange country without even a week's vacation so I hope you can excuse it. The Independence Day celebrations are well under way and everything's been delegated. I'm sure you won't miss me at all." She squeezed the last words out right as she ran out of gumption.

"Not miss you? The Independence Day celebrations are the biggest event in the history of Ruthenia—well, since the 1502 civil war, at least. We can't possibly manage without you, even for a day."

Andi swallowed. He didn't care about her at all, just about the big day coming up. Wasn't it always like this? He was all business, all the time. After six years working together he barely knew anything about her. Which wasn't fair, since she knew almost everything about him. She'd eaten, slept and breathed Jake Mondragon for the past six years and in the process fallen utterly and totally in love with him.

Shame he didn't even notice she was female.

He peered down at her, concern in his brown eyes. "I told you to take some vacation. Didn't I suggest you go back home for a few weeks last summer?"

Home? Where was home anymore? She'd given up her apartment in Manhattan when she moved here. Her parents both worked long hours and had moved to a different suburb since she left high school, so if she went to see them she'd just end up hanging around their house—probably pining for Jake.

Well, no more. She was going to find a new home and start over. She had an interview for a promising job as an event planner scheduled for next week in Manhattan, and that was a perfect next step to going out on her own.

"I don't want to be a personal assistant for the rest of my life and I'm turning twenty-seven soon so it's time to kick-start my career."

"We can change your title. How about…" His dark eyes narrowed. She couldn't help a slight quickening in her pulse. "Chief executive officer."

"Very funny. Except that I'd still be doing all the same things."

"No one else could do them as well as you."

"I'm sure you'll manage." The palace had a staff of nearly thirty including daytime employees. She was hardly leaving him in the lurch. And she couldn't possibly stand to be here for Independence Day next week. The press had made a big deal of how important it was for him to choose a bride; the future of the monarchy depended on it. He'd jokingly given their third Independence Day as his deadline when he'd assumed the crown three years ago.

Now everyone expected him to act on it. Being a man of his word, Andi knew he would. Maxi, Alia, Carina, there were plenty to choose from, and she couldn't bear to see him with any of them.

Jake put down the guest list, but made no move to take her letter of resignation. "I know you've been working hard. Life in a royal palace is a bit of a twenty-four-hour party, but you do get to set your own hours and you've never been shy about asking for good compensation."

"I'm very well paid and I know it." She did pride herself on asking for raises regularly. She knew Jake respected that, which was probably half the reason she'd done it. As a result she had a nice little nest egg put aside to fund her new start. "But it's time for me to move on."

Why was she even so crazy about him? He'd never shown the slightest glimmer of interest in her.

Her dander rose still higher as Jake glanced at his watch. "The guests will be here any minute and I need to return a call from New York. We'll talk later and figure something out." He reached out and clapped her on the arm, as if she was an old baseball buddy. "We'll make you happy."

He turned and left the room, leaving her holding her letter of resignation between trembling fingers.

Once the door had closed behind him, she let out a growl of frustration. Of course he thought he could talk her down and turn everything around. Isn't that exactly what he was known for? And he even imagined he could make her "happy."

That kind of arrogance should be unforgivable.

Except that his endless confidence and can-do attitude were possibly what she admired and adored most in him.

The only way he could make her happy was to sweep her off her feet into a passionate embrace and tell her he loved her and wanted to marry her.

Except that kings didn't marry secretaries from Pittsburgh. Even kings of funny little countries like Ruthenia.

"The vol-au-vents are done, cook's wondering where to send them."

Andi started at the sound of the events assistant coming through another doorway behind her.

"Why don't you have someone bring them up for the first guests? And the celery stalks with the cheese filling." She tucked the letter behind her back.

Livia nodded, her red curls bobbing about the collar of her white shirt, like it was just another evening.

Which of course it was, except that it was Andi's last evening here.

"So did they ask you in for an interview?" Livia leaned in with a conspiratorial whisper.

"I cannot confirm or deny anything of that nature."

"How are you going to manage an interview in New York when you're imprisoned in a Ruthenian palace?"

Andi tapped the side of her nose. She hadn't told anyone she was leaving. That would feel too much like a betrayal of Jake. Let them just wake up to find her gone.

Livia put her hands on her hips. "Hey, you can't just take off back to New York without me. I told you about that job."

"You didn't say you wanted it."

"I said I thought it sounded fantastic."

"Then you should apply." She wanted to get away. This conversation was not productive and she didn't trust Livia to keep her secrets.

Livia narrowed her eyes. "Maybe I will."

Andi forced a smile. "Save a vol-au-vent for me, won't you?"

Livia raised a brow and disappeared back through the door.

Who would be in charge of choosing the menus and how the food should be served? The cook, probably, though she had quite a temper when she felt pressured. Perhaps Livia? She wasn't the most organized person in the palace and she'd been skipped over for promotion a few times. Probably why she wanted to leave.

Either way, it wasn't her problem and Jake would soon find someone to replace her. Her heart clenched at the thought, but she drew in a steadying breath and marched out into the hallway toward the foyer. She could hear the hum of voices as the first guests took off their luxurious coats and handed them to the footmen to reveal slinky evening gowns and glittering jewels.

Andi smoothed the front of her black slacks. It wasn't appropriate for a member of staff to get decked out like a guest.

All eyes turned to the grand staircase as Jake descended to greet the ladies with a kiss on each cheek. Andi tried to ignore the jealousy flaring in her chest. How ridiculous. One of these girls was going to marry him and she had no business being bothered in any way.

"Could you fetch me a tissue?" asked Maxi Rivenshnell. The willowy brunette cast her question in Andi's direction, without actually bothering to meet her gaze.

"Of course." She reached into her pocket and withdrew a folded tissue from the packet she kept on her. Maxi snatched it from her fingers and tucked it into the top of her long satin gloves without a word of thanks.

She didn't exist for these people. She was simply there to serve them, like the large staff serving each of their aristocratic households.

A waiter appeared with a tray of champagne glasses and she helped to distribute them amongst the guests, then ushered people into the green drawing room where a fire blazed in a stone fireplace carved with the family crest.

Jake strolled and chatted with ease as the room filled with well-dressed Ruthenians. Several of them had only recently returned after decades of exile in places like London, Monaco and Rome, ready to enjoy Ruthenia's promised renaissance after decades of failed socialism.

So far the promise was coming true. The rich were getting richer, and—thanks to Jake's innovative business ideas—everyone else was, as well. Even the staunch anti-monarchists who'd opposed his arrival with protests in the streets now had to admit that Jake Mondragon knew what he was doing.

He'd uncovered markets for their esoteric agricultural

products, and encouraged multinational firms to take advantage of Ruthenia's strategic location in central Europe and its vastly underemployed workforce. The country's GDP had risen nearly 400% in just three years, making eyeballs pop all across the globe.

Andi stiffened as Jake's bold laugh carried through the air. She'd miss that sound. Was she really leaving? A sudden flash of panic almost made her reconsider.

Then she followed the laugh to its source and her heart seized as she saw Jake with his arm around yet another Ruthenian damsel—Carina Teitelhaus—whose blond hair hung in a silky sheet almost to her waist.

Andi tugged her gaze away and busied herself with picking up a dropped napkin. She would not miss seeing him draped over other women one bit. He joked that he was just trying to butter up their powerful parents and get them to invest in the country, but right now that seemed like one more example of how people were pawns to him rather than living beings with feelings.

He'd marry one of them just because it was part of his job. And she couldn't bear to see that.

She needed to leave tonight, before he could use his well-practiced tongue to… Thoughts of his tongue sent an involuntary shiver through her.

Which was exactly why she needed to get out of here. And she wasn't going to give him a chance to talk her out of it.

Jake pushed his dessert plate forward. He'd had all the sticky sweetness he could stand for one night. With Maxi on one side and Alia on the other, each vying to tug his attention from the other, he felt exhausted. Andi knew he liked to have at least one decent conversationalist seated next to him, yet she'd followed through on her threat to stick him between two of the most troublesome vixens in Ruthenia.

Speaking of which, where was Andi?

He glanced around the dining room. The flickering light from the candles along the table and walls created deep shadows, but he didn't see her. Usually she hovered close by in case he needed something.

He summoned one of the servers. "Ulrike, have you seen Andi?"

The quiet girl shook her head. "Would you like me to find her, sir?"

"No, thanks, I'll find her myself." At least he would as soon as he could extricate himself from yet another eight-course meal. He couldn't risk offending either of his bejeweled dinner companions with an early departure since their darling daddies were the richest and most powerful men in the region. Once things were settled, he wouldn't have to worry so much about currying their favor, but while the economy was growing and changing and finding its feet in the world, he needed their flowing capital to oil its wheels.

He could see how men in former eras had found it practical to marry more than one woman. They were both pretty—Maxi a sultry brunette with impressive cleavage and Alia a graceful blonde with a velvet voice—but to be completely honest he didn't want to marry either of them.

Carina Teitelhaus shot him a loaded glance from across the table. Her father owned a large factory complex with a lot of potential for expansion. And she didn't hesitate to remind him of that.

Ruthenia's noblewomen were becoming increasingly aggressive in pursuing the role of queen. Lately he felt as if he were juggling a bevy of flaming torches and the work of keeping them all in the air was wearing on his nerves.

He'd committed to choosing a bride before Independence Day next week. At the time he'd made that statement the deadline had seemed impossibly far off and none of them were sure Ruthenia itself would even still be in existence.

Now it was right upon them, along with the necessity of choosing his wife or breaking his promise. Everyone in the room was painfully aware of each glance, every smile or laugh he dispensed in any direction. The dining table was a battlefield, with salvos firing over the silver.

Usually he could count on Andi to soothe any ruffled feathers with careful seating placements and subtly co-ordinated private trysts. Tonight, though, contrary to her promise, she'd left him in the lurch.

"Do excuse me, ladies." He rose to his feet, avoiding all mascara-laden glances, and strode for the door.

Andi's absence worried him. What if she really did leave? She was the anchor that kept the palace floating peacefully in the choppy seas of a changing Ruthenia. He could give her any task and just assume it was done, without a word of prompting. Her tact and thoughtfulness were exemplary, and her organizational skills were unmatched. He couldn't imagine life without her.

After a short walk over the recently installed plum-colored carpets of the west hallway, he glanced into her ever-tidy office—and found it dark and empty. He frowned. She was often there in the evenings, which coincided with business hours in the U.S. and could be a busy time.

Her laptop was on the desk, as usual. That was a good sign.

Jake headed up the west staircase to the second floor, where most of the bedrooms were located. Andi had a large "family" bedroom rather than one of the pokey servants' quarters on the third floor. She was family, dammit. And that meant she couldn't pick up and leave whenever she felt like it.

A nasty feeling gripped his gut as he approached her closed door. He knocked on the polished wood and listened for movement on the other side.

Nothing.

He tried the handle and to his surprise the door swung open. Curiosity tickling his nerves, he stepped inside and switched on the light. Andi's large room was neat and free of clutter—much like her desk. It looked like a hotel room, with no personal touches added to the rather extravagant palace décor. The sight of two black suitcases—open and packed—stopped him in his tracks.

She really was leaving.

Adrenaline surged through him. At least she hadn't gone yet, or the bags would be gone, too. The room smelled faintly of that subtle scent she sometimes wore, almost as if she was in the room with him.

He glanced around. Could she be hiding from him?

He strode across the room and tugged open the doors of the massive armoire. His breath stopped for a second and he half expected to see her crouched inside.

Which of course she wasn't. Her clothes were gone, though, leaving only empty hangers on the rod.

Anger warred with deep disappointment that she intended to abandon him like this. Did their six years together mean nothing to her?

She couldn't leave without her suitcases. Perhaps he should take them somewhere she couldn't find them. His room, for example.

Unfamiliar guilt pricked him. He didn't even like the idea of her knowing he'd entered her room uninvited, let alone taken her possessions hostage. Andi was a stickler for honesty and had kept him aboveboard more times than he cared to remember. Taking her bags just felt wrong.

She'd said she'd leave as soon as the party was over. A woman of her word, she'd be sure to wait until the last guest was gone. As long as he found her before then, everything would be fine. He switched off the light and left the room as he'd found it.

He scanned the east hall as he headed for the stairs, a sense of foreboding growing inside him. The packed bags were an ominous sign, but he couldn't really believe she'd abandon Ruthenia—and him.

"Jake, darling, we were wondering what happened to you," Maxi called to him from the bottom of the stairs. "Colonel Von Deiter has volunteered to play piano while we dance." She stretched out her long arm, as if inviting him to share the first dance with her.

Since coming to Ruthenia he sometimes felt he'd stepped into a schnitzel-flavored Jane Austen story, where people waltzed around ballrooms and gossiped behind fans. He was happier in a business meeting than on a dance floor, and right now he'd much rather be dictating a letter to Andi than twirling Maxi over the parquet.

"Have you seen Andi, my assistant?"

"The little girl who wears her hair in a bun?"

Jake frowned. He wasn't sure exactly how old Andi was—mid-twenties, maybe?—but it seemed a bit rude for someone of twenty-two to call her a little girl. "She's about five foot seven," he said, with an arched brow. "And yes, she always wears her hair in a bun."

Come to think of it, he'd literally never seen her hair down, which was pretty odd after six years. A sudden violent urge to see Andi with her hair unleashed swept through him. "I've looked all over the palace for her, but she's vanished into thin air."

Maxi shrugged. "Do come dance, darling."

His friend Fritz appeared behind her. "Come on, Jake. Can't let the ladies down. Just a twirl or two. I'm sure Andi has better things to do than wait on you hand and foot."

"She doesn't wait on me hand and foot. She's a valued executive."

Fritz laughed. "Is that why she's always hovering around taking care of your every need?"

Jake stiffened. He never took Andi for granted. He knew just how dependent on her he was. Did she feel that he didn't care?

Frowning, he descended the stairs and took Maxi's offered hand. He was the host, after all. Two waltzes and a polka later he managed to slip out into the hallway.

"Any idea where Andi is?" he asked the first person he saw, who happened to be the night butler.

He shrugged in typical Ruthenian style. "Haven't seen her in hours. Maybe she went to bed?"

Unlikely. Andi never left a party until the last guest had rolled down the drive. But then she'd never quit before, either. He was halfway up the stairs before he realized he was heading for her bedroom again.

Jake stared at her closed door. Was she in there? And if not, were her bags still there?

He knocked, but heard no movement from inside. After checking that the corridor was deserted, he knelt and peered through the keyhole. It was empty—no key on the inside—which suggested she was out. On the other hand, the pitch darkness on the other side meant he couldn't see a thing.

He slipped in—didn't she know better than to leave her door unlocked?—and switched on the light. The suitcases were still there. Closer inspection revealed that one of them had been partially unpacked, as if an item was removed. Still, there were no clues as to Andi's whereabouts.

Frustration pricked his muscles. How could she just disappear like this?

At the foot of the stairs, Fritz accosted him, martini in hand. "When are you going to choose your bride, Jake? We're all getting impatient."

Jake growled. "Why is everyone so mad for me to get married?"

"Because there are precious few kings left in the world and you're up for grabs. The rest of us are waiting to see who's left. None of the girls dare even kiss us anymore, let alone do anything more rakish, in case they're making themselves ineligible for a coronet. They're all fighting for the chance to be called Your Majesty."

"Then they're all nuts. If anyone calls *me* 'Your Majesty,' I'll fire 'em."

Fritz shoved him. "All bluster. And don't deny you have some of the loveliest women in the world to choose from."

"I wish the loveliest women in the world would take off for the night. I'm ready to turn in." Or rather, ready to find and corner Andi.

Fritz cocked his head. "Party pooper. All right. I'll round up the troops and march 'em out for you."

"You're a pal."

Jake watched the last chauffeured Mercedes disappear down the long driveway from the east patio. He needed some air to clear his head before tackling Andi—and watching from here ensured that she couldn't leave without him seeing her.

Could he really stand to marry Maxi or Alia or any of these empty-headed, too-rich, spoiled brats? He'd been surrounded by their kind of women all his life, even in New York. Just the circle he'd been born into. You'd think a king would have more choices than the average Joe, but that was apparently not the case.

Something moving in the darkness caught his eye. He squinted, trying to make out what was crossing the lawn. An animal? Ruthenia had quite large deer that he was supposed to enjoy hunting.

But this creature was lighter, more upright, and moved with a kind of mystical grace. He stepped forward, peering into the gloom of a typical moonlit but cloudy night. The figure whirled and twirled on the lawn, pale fabric flowing around it.

A ghost? His back stiffened. The palace was nearly three hundred years old and built over a far more ancient structure. Tales of sieges and beheadings and people imprisoned in the dungeons rattled around the old stone walls.

Long, pale arms extended sideways as the figure twirled again. A female ghost.

Curiosity goaded him across the patio and down the stone stairs onto the lawn. He walked silently across the damp grass, eyes fixed on the strange apparition. As he drew closer he heard singing—soft and sweet—almost lost in the low breeze and the rustling of the trees.

Entranced, he moved nearer, enjoying the figure's graceful movements and the silver magic of her voice.

He stopped dead when he realized she was singing in English.

"Andi?"

Despite the hair streaming over her shoulders and the long, diaphanous dress, he recognized his assistant of six years, arms raised to the moon, swaying and singing in the night.

He strode forward faster. "Are you okay?"

She stopped and stared at him and the singing ceased. Her eyes shone bright in the darkness.

"What are you doing out here?" He walked right up to her, partly to prove to himself that she was real and not a figment of his imagination. His chest swelled with relief. At least now he'd found her and they could have that talk he'd been rehearsing in his head all night.

"Why don't we go inside?" He reached out for her hand, almost expecting his own to pass through it. She still looked so spectral, smiling in the cloud-veiled moonlight.

But the hand that seized his felt warm. Awareness snapped through him as her fingers closed around his. Her hair was longer than he'd imagined. Almost to the peaks of her nipples, which jutted out from the soft dress. He swallowed. He'd never noticed what…luxurious breasts Andi had. They were usually hidden under tailored suits and crisp blouses.

He struggled to get back on task. "We need to talk."

Andi's grip tightened on his, but she didn't move. Her face looked different. Transfixed, somehow. Her eyes sparkling and her lips glossy and parted. Was she drunk?

"You must be cold." On instinct he reached out to touch her upper arm, which was bare in the floaty evening gown she wore. As he drew closer, her free arm suddenly wrapped around his waist with force.

Jake stilled as she lifted her face to his. She smelled of that same soft scent she always wore, not a trace of alcohol, just flowers and sweetness. He groped for words, but failed to find any as her lips rose toward his.

Next thing he knew he was kissing her full—and hard—on the mouth.

Two

Jake let his arms wind around her waist. The movement was as instinctive as breathing. Their mouths melted together and her soft body pressed against his. Desire flared inside him, hot and unexpected, as the kiss deepened. His fingers ached to explore the lush curves she'd kept hidden for so long.

But this was Andi—his faithful and long-suffering assistant, not some bejeweled floozy who just wanted to lock lips with a monarch.

He pulled back from the kiss with great difficulty, unwinding himself from the surprisingly powerful grip of her slim arms. A momentary frown flashed across her lovely face—why had he never noticed she was so pretty?—then vanished again as a smile filled her soft eyes and broadened her mouth.

She lifted a hand and stroked his cheek. "You're beautiful."

Shocked, Jake struggled for a response. "*You're* beautiful. I'm handsome." He lifted a brow, as if to assure himself they were both kidding.

She giggled—in a most un-Andi-like way—and tossed her head, which sent her hair tumbling over her shoulders in a shimmering cascade. She twirled again, and the soft dress draped her form, allowing him a tantalizing view of her figure. He'd certainly never seen her in this dress before. Floor-length and daringly see-through, it was far dressier and more festive than her usual attire.

"Happiness is glorious joy," she sang, as she turned to face him again.

"Huh?" Jake frowned.

"Mysterious moonlight and wonderful wishes." Another silver peal of laughter left her lips—which looked quite different than he remembered, bare of their usual apricot lipstick and kissed to ruby fullness.

Unless she'd suddenly turned to poetry—very bad poetry at that—she must be intoxicated. He didn't smell anything on her breath, though. And didn't she always insist she was allergic to alcohol? He couldn't remember ever seeing her with a real drink.

Drugs?

He peered at her eyes. Yes, her pupils were dilated. Still, Andi experimenting with illegal substances? It seemed impossible.

"Did you take something?"

"Steal? I'd never steal from you. You're my true love." She gazed at him as she spoke the words, eyes clear and blue as a summer sky.

Jake groped for words. "I meant, did you take any pills?"

You're my true love? She was obviously tripping on something. He'd better get her inside before she tried to fly from the parapets or walk on the water in the moat. "Let's go inside."

He wrapped his arm around her, and she squeezed against him and giggled again. This was not the Andi he knew. Perhaps the stress of threatening to leave had encouraged her to take some kind of tranquilizer. He had no idea how those things worked, but couldn't come up with any other explanation for her odd behavior.

"You smell good." She pressed her face against him, almost tripping him.

Jake's eyes widened, but he managed to keep walking. Her body bumping against his was not helping his own sanity. Now she'd slid an arm around his waist and her fingers fondled him as they walked. His blood was heating in a most uncomfortable way.

Maybe he could bring both of them back down to earth.

"It was cold of you to seat me between Maxi and Alia."

"Who?" She marched gaily along over the lawn, still clinging to him. No reaction to the names.

"Maxi and Alia. Both of them fighting over me was a bit much to take on top of the cook's roulade."

"Pretty names. We haven't met. You must introduce me sometime." She pulled her arm from his waist and took off skipping across the damp lawn.

Jake paused and stared for a moment, then strode after her.

Since he didn't particularly want any of the other staff to see Andi in this compromising state, Jake hustled her into his private chambers and locked the door. That was the accepted signal that he was off duty for the night and not to be disturbed.

Andi made herself quite at home, curling up on one

of the sofas, with a languid arm draping along the back. "Happiness is as happiness does," she said dreamily.

Jake resisted the urge to pour himself a whisky. "Listen, what you said about leaving. I saw your bags—"

"Leave? I would never leave you, my love." Her face rested in a peaceful smile.

Jake swallowed. "So you're staying."

"Of course. Forever and ever and ever." Her eyes sparkled.

"Ah. That's settled then." He moved to the liquor cabinet, deciding to have that whisky after all. "I am relieved. The thought of managing without you was quite frightening."

Andi had risen from the sofa and was now waltzing around the room by herself, singing, "Someday my prince will come." She twirled, sweeping her pale evening dress about her like smoke. "Some day I'll love someone." Her radiant smile was almost infectious.

Almost. Jake took a swig of his drink. Did she really think they were having some kind of relationship outside their well-established professional one? As much as the idea appealed right this second, he knew it would really mess things up once she snapped out of whatever chemical induced trance she was in.

He'd better remind her of that. "We've worked together a long time."

She stopped twirling for a moment, and frowned. "I don't think I do work."

"You're a lady of leisure?"

She glanced down at her evening gown. "Yes." She frowned; then her expression brightened. "I must be. Otherwise why would I be dressed like this?"

Had she temporarily forgotten that she was his assistant? "Why are you dressed like that?" She'd certainly never worn anything so festive before.

"It's pretty, isn't it?" She looked up at him. "Do you like it?"

"Very much." He allowed his eyes to soak up the vision of it draped over her gorgeous body. Desire licked through him in tiny, tormenting flames.

Andi reached out and tugged at his shirt. Even that made his synapses flash and his groin tighten.

"Why don't you come sit with me." She stroked the sofa cushion next to her.

"I'm not sure that's a good idea." His voice came out gruff.

"Why not?"

"It's late. We should get to bed." The image of her in his bed flooded his brain, especially as it was right there in the next room. But caution tightened his muscles.

"Oh, don't be silly—" She frowned. "How odd." She glanced up at him. "I can't think of your name right now."

Jake was about to tell her, but something made him stop. "You don't know my name?"

She looked up for a few moments, as if searching her brain. "No, I don't seem to know it."

Panic tightened his chest. "What's your name?"

She looked toward the ceiling, scrunched up her brow and clenched her fists. When she finally looked back at him, her expression had changed from glee to confusion. "I'm not sure."

"I think we should call for a doctor." He pulled his phone out.

"A doctor? What for? I feel fine."

He hesitated. "Let me look at you. Did you bump your head?"

She shrugged. "I don't think so."

He put his phone back in his pocket and touched her temples with his thumbs. Her eyes sparkled as she looked up at him and her scent was a torment. He worked his fingers gently back into her hair—which was soft and luxurious to touch. "Hey, I feel a lump."

"Ouch!"

"You have a bruise." He touched it gently. A big goose egg. That explained a whole lot. "We're definitely calling the doctor. You could have a concussion." He dialed the number. "Listen, sorry it's so late, Gustav, but Andi's taken a fall and bumped her head. She's not talking too much sense and I think you should look at her."

Gustav replied that he'd be there in the ten minutes it took to drive from the town, and to keep her awake until he got there.

After letting the staff know to expect Gustav, Jake sat down on the sofa opposite her. It made sense to find out just how much of her memory had vanished. "How old are you?" Odd that he didn't know that.

"Over twenty-one." She laughed. Then frowned. "Other than that, I'm not too sure. How old do I look?"

Jake smiled. "I'd be a damned fool if I answered a question like that from a woman." He decided he'd be better off following the lawyer's strategy of only asking questions he knew the answer to. It was pretty embarrassing that he really didn't know how old she was. "How long have you lived here?"

She stared at him, mouth slightly open, then looked away. "Why are you asking me these silly questions? I've lived here a long time. With you."

Her gaze—innocent yet needy—ate into him. She stroked the sofa arm with her fingers and his skin tingled in response. She seemed to have lost her memory, and, in its absence, assumed they were a couple.

Jake sucked in a long breath. They'd never had any kind of flirtation, even a playful one. She always seemed so businesslike and uninterested in such trivial matters. He'd never really looked at her that way, either. Much simpler to keep business and pleasure separate, especially when a really good assistant was so hard to find and keep.

Right now he was seeing a different aspect of Andi— alarming, and intriguing.

She rose and walked a few steps to his sofa, then sank down next to him. Her warm thigh settled against his, causing his skin to sizzle even through their layers of clothing. He stiffened. Was it fair to offer a man this kind of temptation?

At least it was keeping her awake.

Her fingers reached up to his black bow tie and tugged at one end. The knot came apart and the silk ribbons fell to his starched shirtfront.

"Much better." She giggled again, then pulled the tie out from his collar and undid the top button of his shirt. Jake watched, barely breathing, trying to suppress the heaving tide of arousal surging inside him.

After all, it would be rude to push her away, wouldn't it? Especially in her delicate and mysterious condition.

When her fingers roamed into his hair, causing his groin to ache uncomfortably, he had to take action. He stood up rapidly. "The doctor will be here any minute. Can I get you a glass of water?"

"I'm not thirsty." Her hurt look sent a pang to his heart.

"Still, it's good to keep hydrated." He busied himself with filling a glass at the bar, and took care not to accidentally brush her fingertips as he handed it to her. Her cheeks and lips were flushed with pink, which made her look aroused and appealing at the same time.

She took the glass and sipped cautiously. Then looked up at him with a slight frown. "I do feel odd."

Jake let out a sigh of relief. This seemed more like the real Andi than the one spouting loopy epithets. "You'll probably feel better in the morning, but it can't hurt to have the doctor take a look."

Alarm filled him as tears welled in her eyes. "It's just so strange not being able to remember anything. How could I not even know my own name?" A fat tear rolled down her soft cheek.

Disturbing that he now knew how soft her cheek was.

"Your name is Andi Blake."

"Andi." She said it softly. Then frowned again. "Is that short for something?"

Jake froze. Was it? He had no idea. He didn't remember ever calling her anything else, but it had been six long years since he'd seen her résumé and frankly he couldn't remember the details. "Nope. Just Andi. It's a pretty name."

He regretted the lame comment, something you might say to a six-year-old. But then he didn't have experience in dealing with amnesiacs, so maybe it wasn't all that inappropriate.

"Oh." She seemed to mull that over. She wiped her eyes. "At least I know my own name now." Then she bit her lip. "Though it doesn't sound at all familiar." Tears glistened in her eyes. "What if my memory doesn't come back?"

"Don't worry about that, I'm sure—" A knock on the door announced the arrival of the doctor, and Jake released a sigh of relief. "Please send him in."

Andi's tearful trembling subsided as the doctor checked her over, peering into her eyes with a light, checking her pulse and breathing, and taking her temperature.

As the local doctor, he'd been to the palace before and knew Andi. She showed no sign of recognizing or remembering him. His questions revealed that while she remembered general concepts, like how to tie a knot, she recalled nothing about her own life.

"Andi, would you excuse us a moment?" The doctor ushered Jake out into the hallway. "Is she exhibiting mood changes?"

"Big time. She's not like herself at all. She seemed happy—silly even—when I first found her. Just now she was crying. I think the reality of what's going on is setting in."

"Sounds like a pretty textbook case of temporary memory loss, if there is such a thing." The older man snapped his briefcase closed. "Lots of emotion. Mood swings. Loss of long-term memory. I've never seen it before, myself, but in most cases the memory eventually starts to come back."

"When? How long will she be like this?"

The doctor gave a Ruthenian shrug. "Could be days, could be weeks. There's a slim possibility she won't ever recall everything. She's certainly had a good bump to her head, but no signs of concussion or other injury. Do you have any idea what happened?"

Jake shook his head. "I found her out dancing on the lawn. I didn't see anything happen at all."

"Make sure she gets plenty of sleep, and encourage her with questions to bring back her memory." The doctor hoisted his bag onto his shoulder. "Call me anytime, of course."

"Thanks." Jake frowned. "Can we keep this amnesia thing between us? I think Andi would be embarrassed if people knew what was going on. She's a very private person."

The doctor's brow furrowed even more than usual. "Of course." *Your Highness.* The unspoken words hovered in the air. Jake sensed slight disapproval at his request for secrecy, but he knew the physician would honor it. "Please keep me posted on her progress."

Jake went back into his suite and locked the door. Andi was sitting on the sofa and her mood seemed to have brightened. Her tears were gone, and a smile hovered in her eyes as she looked up at him. "Will I live?"

"Without a doubt. It's late. How about some sleep?"

"I'm not at all sleepy." She draped herself over the sofa, eyes heavy-lidded with desire. "I'd rather play."

Jake's eyes widened. Could this really be the same Andi he'd worked with all these years? It was shocking to imagine that this flirtatious person had been lurking inside her the whole time. Unless it was just a mood swing caused by her condition.

She rose from the sofa and swept toward him, then threw her arms around his waist. "I do love you."

Gulp. Jake patted her cautiously on the back. This could last for days. Or weeks. Or longer.

His skin tingled as her lips pressed against his cheek. "I'm so glad we're together." Her soft breath heated his skin as she breathed the words in his ear.

And this was the woman who'd announced, only a few hours before, that she was leaving for good, that night.

At least that was off the agenda for now.

His phone rang and he tensed. What now? "Excuse me." He extricated himself from her embrace and pulled it from his pocket.

A glance at the number revealed the caller was Maxi. She'd formed a new habit of calling him at bizarre times like the crack of dawn or during his morning workout. This call in the wee hours was a new and even more unappealing attempt to monopolize his time.

Still, maybe there was some kind of emergency.

"Hi, Maxi."

"Jake, are you still awake?" Her breathy voice grated on his nerves.

"I am now." He glanced at Andi, who was twirling around the room doing the dance of the seven veils, or something. "What do you want?"

"So impatient. I just wanted to chat. About you and me."

He shoved a hand through his hair. Maxi was definitely not The One. In fact she could be voted Least Likely to be Queen of Ruthenia, since she was firmly in his "keep your enemies closer" circle. He'd been drawing her in and inviting her confidence on purpose. Not because he loved her, or was even attracted to her. He'd found evidence that her family was involved in weapons dealing and possibly worse, but he didn't have enough proof to do anything about it yet.

None of the other girls dealt in arms or drugs, as far as he knew, but they were all empty-headed and silly. Right now he was more attracted to his own assistant than to any of Ruthenia's pampered beauties.

An idea crept into his brain.

Since Andi seemed to assume they were a couple, why not make it a reality? He had to marry someone. He could announce to the press tomorrow that his chosen bride was his own assistant.

A chill of sangfroid crept over him. Could he really arrange his own marriage so easily? Andi was agreeable, intelligent and practical, perfectly suited to life in the spotlight. She'd worked just outside it for years and knew the whole routine of palace life perfectly. Apart from her presumably humble origins—he really didn't know anything about her origins, but since he'd never met her parents at a ball, he was guessing—she'd be the ideal royal wife.

They'd known each other for years and he could simply

announce that they'd been involved for a long time but kept their relationship secret.

The announcement would send the long-fingernailed wolves away from his door for good. He and Andi could marry, produce an heir and a spare or two, and live a long, productive life in the service of the citizens of Ruthenia— wasn't that what was really important?

Andi had wandered into the bedroom and a quick glance revealed that she now lay sprawled on his bed.

Heat surged through him like a shot of brandy.

Her dress draped over her, displaying her inviting curves like an ice-cream sundae with whipped cream on top. Her gaze beckoned him, along with her finger. His muscles itched to join her on the bed and enjoy discovering more of Andi's wickedly intriguing sensual side.

"Maxi, I have to go. Have a good night."

"I can think of a way to have a much better night."

Jake's flesh crawled. "Sleep knits up the raveled sleeve of care."

"Is that Moby?"

"Shakespeare. Goodnight, Maxi."

"When are you going to choose your wife?" Jake flinched at the blunt question, and the shrill voice that asked it. "Daddy wants to know. He's not sure whether to contribute funds for the new hydroelectric project."

Jake stiffened. This is what it all boiled down to. Money and power. Well, he didn't want to build Ruthenia with ill-gotten gains from the black market, and he'd rather share his life with a hardworking woman than one who thought she could buy her way into a monarchy. "I've already chosen my wife."

"What do you mean?" she gasped.

He moved across the room, away from the bedroom where Andi now sprawled enticingly on the bed. She was humming again, and wouldn't hear him. "I intend to marry Andi Blake, my longtime assistant."

"You're joking."

"Not in the slightest. She and I have had a close relationship for six years. We intend to enjoy each other's company for many more."

Already his pronouncement had an official ring to it. Marriage to Andi was a perfectly natural and practical course of action. He was confident Andi would agree, especially since she seemed to have romantic feelings toward him.

"People are going to be very, very..." She paused, apparently struggling for words.

"Happy for us. Yes. Of course you'll be invited to the wedding." He couldn't help a tiny smile sneaking across his mouth. Maxi had clearly intended to be the featured host of the event.

"Invited to the wedding?" Her growl made him pull the phone away from his ear. "You're impossible!"

The dial tone made a satisfying noise. And now he wouldn't have to even make an announcement. Maxi would do all the legwork for him.

All he had to do was tell Andi.

Three

Morning sunlight streamed through the gap between heavy brocade curtains. Hot and uncomfortable, Andi looked down to find herself wearing a long evening dress under the covers. Weirdest thing, she had no idea why.

She sat bolt upright. Where was she?

His room. She remembered the soft touch of his lips on her cheek. Her skin heated at the memory. "Good night, Andi," he'd said. So she was Andi.

Andi.

Who was Andi? She racked her brain, but the racks were empty. She couldn't even remember the name of the handsome man who'd put her to bed, though she knew they were close.

How could her whole reality just slip away? Her heart pounded and she climbed out of bed. Her chiffon-y dress was horribly wrinkled and had made an uncomfortable nightgown, leaving lines printed on her skin.

She moved to the window and pulled one of the heavy drapes aside. The view that greeted her was familiar—rolling green hills dotted with grazing sheep, rising to fir-covered mountains. The village in the middle distance, with its steep clay-tiled roofs and high church steeple.

Looking down she saw the long rectangular fishpond in the walled courtyard. She didn't recall seeing it from this angle before.

But then she didn't recall much.

Andi what? She pressed a hand to her forehead. Blake, he'd said. How could even her own last name sound alien and unfamiliar?

She walked to the door and cautiously pulled it open. She caught her breath at the sight of him, standing in front of the mirror, buttoning his collar. Thick black-brown hair swept back from the most handsome face she'd ever seen. Warm, dark eyes reflected in the glass. Mouth set in a serious but good-humored line. Heat flooded her body and she stood rooted to the spot.

He turned. "Morning, Andi. How are you feeling?"

His expression looked rather guarded.

"Okay. I think. I…I can't seem to remember much." Had she slept with him last night? Her fully dressed state seemed to suggest not. Her body was sending all kinds of strange signals, though—pulsing and throbbing and tingling in mysterious places—so she couldn't tell.

"What can you remember?" He didn't look surprised at her announcement. Did he know what was going on?

"Why can't I remember?"

He took a few steps toward her and put his hand on her arm. Arousal flashed through her at his touch. "You bumped your head. The doctor says you're not concussed."

"How long have I been like this?" Fear twisted in her stomach.

"Just since last night. The doc said your memory will come back soon. A few weeks at most."

"Oh." Andi frowned, feeling ridiculously vulnerable, standing there in her wrinkled dress with no idea of who or where she was. Except that she was very—very—attracted to this man. "What should I do in the meantime?"

"Don't worry about a thing. I'll take care of you." He stroked her cheek. The reassuring touch of his fingers made her breath catch and sent tingles of arousal cascading through her.

She frowned. How should she put a question like this? "Are we…intimate?"

His gaze flickered slightly, making her stomach tighten. Had she said the wrong thing? She felt sure there must be something between them. She remembered kissing him last night, and the memory of the kiss made her head grow light.

"Yes, Andi. We're going to be married." He looked down at her hands, gathering them in his.

"Oh." She managed a smile. "What a relief that I have you to take care of me until my memory comes back." If it did come back. "It's embarrassing to ask, but how long have we been together?"

"Oh, years." He met her gaze again.

"It seems impossible, but I don't remember your name."

"Jake." He looked slightly flustered, and why wouldn't he? "Jake Mondragon."

"Jake Mondragon." She smiled dreamily, allowing herself to relax in his sturdy presence. And his face was kind, despite the proud, sculpted features. Totally gorgeous, too. She was very lucky. "So I'm going to be Andi Mondragon."

Jake's eyes widened. "Uh, yes. Yes, you are."

Why did he seem surprised by the idea? It was hardly an odd one if they'd been together for years. "Or was I going to keep my original surname?" Curiosity pricked her.

He smiled. "I don't think we'd discussed whether you would change it or not."

"Oh." Funny they hadn't talked about that. After all, what would the children be called? "How long have we been engaged?"

He lifted his chin slightly. "Just since yesterday. We haven't even told anyone yet."

Yesterday? Her eyes widened. "How odd that I would lose my memory on the same day. I can't even remember the proposal."

She watched his Adam's apple move as he swallowed. He must be upset that she couldn't even remember such a momentous and important moment. "I'm sure it will come back eventually."

An odd sensation started forming in the pit of her stomach. Something felt…off. How could she have forgotten her own fiancé? It was disorienting to know less about her own life than someone else did. "I think I should lay low for a few days. I don't really want to see anyone until I know who I am."

Jake grimaced. "I'm afraid that's going to be hard. The media will probably want an interview."

"About my memory?"

"About our engagement."

"Why would we tell the media?"

Jake hesitated for a moment. "Since I'm the king of this country, everything I do is news."

Andi's mouth fell open. "You're the king?" She was pretty sure she wasn't some kind of royal princess or aristocrat. She certainly didn't feel like one. But maybe that explained the long evening gown. She glanced down at its crumpled folds. "How did we meet?"

Jake's lids lowered slightly. "You're my longtime assistant. We just decided to marry."

She blinked. That explained all the sizzling and tingling in her body—she'd been intimate with this man for a long time. How bizarre that she had to hear about her own life from someone else. From the man she'd apparently dated for years and planned to marry.

Then again, if she'd been seeing this man for years, why did his mere presence send shivers of arousal tingling over her skin and zapping through her insides?

A deep breath didn't help clear the odd mix of confusion and emptiness in her brain. She hoped her memory would return before she did anything to embarrass him. "I guess I should get changed. I feel silly asking this, but where are my clothes?"

Jake froze for a moment, brow furrowed. "You wait here. I'll bring some for you."

"It's okay, I don't want to put you to any trouble. If you'll just tell me where they are." She hated feeling so helpless.

"It's no trouble at all. Just relax on the sofa for a bit. I'll be right back."

She shrugged. "I suppose you probably know what I like to wear better than I do. Still, I could come with you. I need to figure out where everything is."

"Better that you get dressed first. I'll be right back."

He left the room abruptly, leaving Andi uneasy. Why was he so anxious for her to stay here? Like he didn't want anyone to see her. Maybe he didn't want people to know about her loss of memory.

She glanced around the room, already feeling alone and worried without him. Did he have to leave? As the king, you'd think he'd just call for a servant to bring her clothes.

Or did things not work that way anymore? When your memory had taken flight it was hard to distinguish between fairy tales and ordinary life.

She lay back on the sofa and tried to relax. She was engaged to a handsome and caring man that she was fiercely attracted to. Maybe her real life was a fairy tale?

Jake strode along the corridor, hoping he wouldn't run into anyone—which was an unfamiliar feeling for him. Usually he prided himself on being up-front and open, but right now he didn't want anyone to know Andi had been about to leave.

That felt…personal.

He was confident she'd keep it to herself until she'd squared things with him. She'd proved over the years that she was the soul of discretion and confided in no one.

Her job was her life. At least it had been until she decided she'd had enough of it. Hurt flared inside him that she could even consider abandoning him and Ruthenia, especially now he'd realized she was the ideal wife for him. This odd memory loss would give him a chance to turn things around and keep her here for good.

He reached her door and slipped into the room with a sense of relief. Her packed suitcases still sat on the floor next to the bed. He closed the door and began to unpack, hanging the clothes back in the closet and placing some items in the large dresser. He intended to make it look as if she'd never thought of leaving.

Some things startled him. A lacy pink nightgown. A pair of black stockings and garters. When had she had occasion to wear these? He didn't think she had been on a single date since they'd moved to Ruthenia.

Guilt speared him at the thought. She was so busy working she had no life at all outside of her job. Why had he assumed that would be enough for her?

He placed her toiletries back in the bathroom. Handling her shampoo bottle and deodorant felt oddly intimate, like he was peeking into her private life. She had a lot of different lipsticks and he tried to arrange them upright on the bathroom shelf, though really he had no idea how she kept them.

She looked a lot prettier without all that lipstick on. Maybe he should just ditch them and she'd be none the wiser?

No. These were her possessions and that would be wrong.

He arranged her eyeliner pencils and powders and bottles of makeup on the shelf, too. Did all women have so much of this stuff? She had a ridiculous assortment of hair products, too—gels and sprays and mousses—which was funny since her hair was almost always tied back in a bun.

It took a full twenty minutes to get her bags unpacked and rearranged in some sort of convincing order. He shoved the bags under the bed and stood back to admire his handiwork.

Too perfect. He pulled a pair of panty hose from a drawer and draped them over the bed. Better.

He was about to leave when he remembered he was supposed to bring her back something to wear. Hmm. Mischief tickled his insides. What would he like to see her in? Not one of those stiff, bright suits she always wore.

He pulled a pair of jeans from one of the drawers. He'd never seen her in those, so why not? A blue long-sleeved T-shirt seemed to match, and he pulled some rather fetching black lace underwear—tags still attached—from the drawer.

He removed the tags. Why not let her think she wore stuff like this every day?

He rolled the items in a soft blue-and-gray sweater and set off down the corridor again, glancing left and right, glad that the palace was still quiet at this hour.

Andi's uncharacteristically anxious face greeted him as he returned to his rooms. She seemed quite different from last night, when she was spouting garbled poetry and dancing around the room. Now she sat curled up on the sofa, clutching her knees.

"How are you feeling?" Her rigid posture made him want to soothe and relax her.

"Nervous. It's odd not knowing anything about myself or my life. More than odd. Scary."

Jake tried to ignore the trickle of guilt that slid down his spine. He had no intention of telling her the truth about her plans to leave. And come to think of it, he hadn't seen any tickets or itineraries in her room. Maybe her plans weren't all that firm, anyway. "Don't worry. It'll all come back eventually. In the meantime, we'll just carry on as usual. Does that sound okay?"

She nodded.

"I brought some clothes." He set them down on the sofa beside him.

She unrolled the sweater and her eyes widened briefly at the sight of the lacy bra and panties. "Thanks."

She glanced up at him, and then at the pile of clothes again.

He resisted a powerful urge to see her slip into that sexy underwear. "You can change in the bedroom if you want some privacy. There are fresh towels in the bathroom if you'd like to take a shower."

Andi closed the bedroom door behind her. If Jake was her fiancé, why did the thought of changing in front of him make her want to blush crimson? She'd probably done it numerous times in the past. This whole situation was so weird. Her own fiancé felt—not like a stranger, but not like an intimate companion, either.

Must be pretty uncomfortable for Jake, too, though he didn't seem too flustered. Maybe he was just the sort to take things in stride. He had a reassuring air of composure, which was probably a good thing in a king.

Andi slipped out of her crumpled evening gown and climbed into a luxurious marble shower that could accommodate about six people. Unlike the scenery outside the window, and even the dressing room/sitting area, which felt at least somewhat familiar, everything in the bathroom suite seemed totally strange, like she'd literally never been there before. Maybe the memory was selective like that in its recall.

The warm water soothed and caressed her and she dried off feeling fresher.

She managed to arrange her hair into some semblance of order using a black comb, and applied some rather masculine-scented deodorant. They obviously didn't share this bathroom as there were no girly items in here at all. Unease pricked her skin again. No real reason for it though. Probably plenty of engaged couples slept in separate rooms. And one would expect extra attention to propriety in a royal household.

The black underwear he'd brought made her want to blush again. Why? It was her own, so why did it feel too racy for her? The bra fit perfectly, and the panties, while very low-cut, were comfortable, too. She was glad to quickly cover them with the practical jeans and blue T-shirt. No socks or shoes? Well, she could go retrieve those herself. She tied the soft sweater around her shoulders and stepped outside.

Jake's mouth broadened into a smile at the sight of her. "You look great." His dark eyes shone with approval.

She shrugged. Something about the ensemble felt funny. Too casual, maybe. It didn't seem right to wear jeans in a royal palace.

"You didn't bring any shoes." She pointed to her bare feet.

"Maybe I wanted to admire your pretty toes."

Heat flared inside her as his gaze slid down her legs to the toes in question. She giggled, feeling suddenly lighthearted. "My toes would still like to find some shoes to hide in. Why wasn't I wearing any last night? I looked in the bedroom and the dressing room, but I didn't see any."

"I don't know." Jake's expression turned more serious. "You were twirling barefoot on the lawn when I found you."

Andi's skin prickled with unease again. "So we decided to get engaged, and then I lost my memory?"

Jake nodded. His guarded expression didn't offer much reassurance.

He took a step toward her. "Don't worry, we'll get through this together." He slid his arms around her waist. Heat rippled in her belly. His scent stirred emotions and sensations and she softened into his embrace. She wondered if he was going to say he loved her, but he simply kissed her softly on the mouth.

Pleasure crept over her. "I guess I'm lucky it happened right here, and that I'm not wandering around some strange place with no idea who I am like those stories you see on the news."

"It is fortunate, isn't it?" He kissed her again. This time both their eyes slid closed and the kiss deepened. Colors swirled and sparkled behind Andi's eyelids and sensation crashed through her, quickening her pulse and making her breath come in unsteady gasps. Her fingers itched to touch the skin under his starched shirt.

She stepped back, blinking, once they managed to pull apart. Were their kisses always this intense?

Jake smiled, relaxed and calm. Apparently this was all par for the course. Andi patted her hair, wishing she could feel half as composed as he looked. Terror snapped through her at the prospect of facing strangers and trying to pretend everything was normal. "Can we keep our engagement a secret for now?"

Jake's eyes widened for a second. "Why?"

"Just so I don't have to answer a lot of questions when I don't even know who I am."

He frowned. "I'm afraid it's too late. I told someone on the phone last night."

"Who?" Not that she'd even know the name.

"Maxi Rivenshnell. She's a…friend of the family."

Andi paused. The name had a nasty ring to it. Maybe it was the way he pronounced it, like something that tasted bad. "Maybe she won't tell anyone."

"I suspect she'll tell everyone." He turned and strode across the room. Shoved a hand through his dark hair. Then he turned and approached her. "But nothing's going to stop me buying you a ring today, and you're going to choose it. First, let me summon your shoes."

Jake parked his Mercedes in his usual reserved spot in the town's main square. No need for chauffeurs and armed escorts in tiny Ruthenia. He rushed around the car to help Andi out, but she was already on her feet and closing the door by the time he got there.

She'd devoured her breakfast of fruit and pastries in the privacy of his suite. At least he knew what she liked to eat. Despite obvious confusion over little things like how to find her way around, she seemed healthy and relatively calm, which was a huge relief.

Of course her reluctance to announce their engagement was a slight hitch in his plans to unload his unwanted admirers, but word would get out soon enough. Ruthenia had more than its share of gossiping busybodies, and for once they'd be working in his favor.

He took her arm and guided her across the main square. Morning sunlight illuminated the old stone facades of the shops and glinted off the slate tiles of the church steeple. Pigeons gathered near the fountain, where a little girl tossed bread crumbs at them and two dogs barked a happy greeting as their owners stopped for a chat.

"The local town," murmured Andi.

"Does it look familiar?"

"A little. Like I've seen it in a dream rather than in real life. It's so pretty."

"It is lovely. You and I saw it together for the first time three years ago."

She paused. "You didn't grow up here?"

"No, I grew up in the States, like you. I didn't come here until the socialist government collapsed in a heap of corruption scandals and people started agitating for the return of the royal family. At first I thought they were nuts, then I realized I could probably help put the country back on its feet." He looked at her, her clear blue eyes wide, soaking in everything he said. "I couldn't have done it without you."

His chest tightened as he spoke the words. All true. Andi's quiet confidence and brisk efficiency made almost anything possible. The prospect of carrying on without her by his side was unthinkable.

"Was I good at being your assistant?" Her serious gaze touched him. "I don't remember anything about my job."

"Exemplary. You've been far more than my assistant. My right-hand woman is a better description."

She looked pleased. "I guess that's a good thing, since we're getting married."

"Absolutely." Jake swallowed. How would she react when her memory returned and she realized they were never romantically involved? He drew in a breath. She wasn't in love with him. Still, she was sensible enough to see that marriage between them would be in the best interests of Ruthenia.

And that kiss had been surprisingly spicy. In fact, he couldn't remember experiencing anything like it in his fairly substantial kissing experience.

Maybe it was the element of the forbidden. He'd never considered kissing his assistant and it still felt...wrong. Probably because it was wrong of him to let her think they'd been a couple. But once a ring was on her finger, they really would be engaged and everything would be on the up and up.

At least until her memory came back.

"The jeweler is down this street." He led her along a narrow cobbled alley barely wide enough for a cart. The kind of street he'd have to fold in his wing mirrors to drive down without scraping the ancient walls on either side. Thick handblown glass squares glazed the bowed window of the shop, giving a distorted view of the luxurious trinkets inside.

Despite its old-world ambience—or maybe because of it—this jeweler was one of the finest in Europe and had recently regained its international reputation as part of Jake's Rediscover Ruthenia campaign. He'd bought quite a few pieces here—gifts for foreign diplomats and wealthy Ruthenian acquaintances. Why had it never occurred to him to buy something lovely for Andi?

He opened the heavy wood door and ushered her in, unable to resist brushing her waist with his fingers as he coaxed her through. The formally attired proprietor rushed forward to greet them. "Welcome, sir." Jake was grateful the man remembered his aversion to pompous titles. "How can we assist you today? A custom commission, perhaps?"

Jake hesitated. Andi might well like a ring designed to her exact specifications—but he needed a ring on her finger right now to make an honest man of him. He certainly didn't want her memory coming back before the setting was tooled. "I suspect you have something lovely in the shop already."

He took Andi's hand in his. It was warm, and he squeezed it to calm her nerves. "We're looking for an engagement ring."

The elderly jeweler's eyes opened wide. His gaze slid to Andi, then back again. He seemed unsure what to make of the situation. Perhaps he'd been following the local gossip columns and was already designing one with Maxi or Alia in mind. "Should I be offering you my congratulations?"

"Most certainly." Jake slid his arm around Andi.

"Wonderful." The jeweler bowed his head slightly in Andi's direction. "My best wishes for you both. And in time for Independence Day, too." A smile creased his wrinkled face. "The whole nation will be overjoyed. I do think a custom creation would be most appropriate. Perhaps with the family crest?"

"Why don't we take a look at what you have in stock?" He tightened his arm around Andi's waist, then loosened it, suddenly aware of how intent he was to hold on to her. Not that she was resisting. She leaned into him, perhaps seeking reassurance he was happy to provide.

A large tray of sparkling rings appeared from a deep wooden cabinet. Jake glanced at Andi and saw her eyes widen.

"See if anything appeals to you." He spoke softly,

suddenly feeling the intimacy of the moment. The first step in their journey through life as a married couple. The rings were nearly all diamonds, some single and some triple, with a large stone flanked by two smaller stones. A few more had clusters of diamonds and there was a large sapphire and a square cut ruby.

Andi drew in a long breath, then reached for a small single diamond in a carved platinum band. She held it for a moment, then extended her fingers to try it on. "Wow, this feels weird. Like you should be doing it, or something." She glanced shyly at him.

Jake swallowed. He took the ring from her—the diamond was too small, anyway—and gingerly slid it onto her slender finger. His skin tingled as he touched hers and a flutter of something stirred in his chest. The ring fit well and looked pretty on her hand.

"What do you think?" She turned her hand, and the stone sparkled in the light.

"Nice." He didn't want to criticize, if that was her choice.

The jeweler frowned. "It's a fine ring, but for the royal family, perhaps something a bit more…extravagant?" He lifted a dramatic large stone flanked by several smaller stones. The kind of ring that would make people's eyes pop. Jake had to admit it was more appropriate under the circumstances.

Andi allowed the older man to slide her choice off her finger and push the big sparkler onto it. His face creased into a satisfied smile as it slid perfectly into place. "Lovely. Much more suitable for a royal bride, if you don't mind my saying."

She tilted her hand to the side and studied the ring. Despite the large size of the stones it also looked elegant on her graceful hands. Jake wondered how he'd never noticed what pretty hands she had. He'd been watching them type his letters and organize his files for years.

"It's a bit over the top...." She paused, still staring at it. "But it is pretty." She looked up at Jake. "What do you think?"

"Very nice." He intended to buy her many more trinkets and baubles to enjoy. It was worth it to see the sunny smile on her face, and they were supporting the local economy. "Let's buy it and go get a hot chocolate to celebrate."

She hesitated for a moment more, studying the ring on her finger. When she looked up, confusion darkened the summer-blue of her eyes. She seemed like she wanted to say something, but hesitated in front of the jeweler. The shop owner tactfully excused himself and disappeared through a low door into a back room.

"I guess he trusts us alone with the merchandise." Jake grinned. "There must be a million dollars worth of rocks on this tray."

"I'd imagine a crown inspires a certain amount of trust." She looked up at him, eyes sparkling. "I'm still getting used to the idea that you're a king."

"Me, too. I'm not sure I'll ever be completely used to it, but at least it's starting to feel like a suit that fits. How does the ring feel?"

Andi studied the ring again. "It is lovely, but it's just so... big."

"He's right, though. It makes sense to go dramatic. Do you want people muttering that I'm a cheapskate?" He raised a brow.

Andi chuckled. "I guess you have a good point." Then she frowned. "Are people going to be shocked that you're marrying your assistant?" She bit her lip for a moment. "I mean...did they know that we're...intimate?"

Jake inhaled. "We kept it all pretty private."

"Did anyone know?" Her serious expression tugged at him.

"A few people may have guessed something." Who knew what people might imagine, even if there had never been anything to guess? "But on the whole, we were discreet so it'll be a surprise."

Andi's shoulders tightened a bit. "I hope they won't be too upset that you're not marrying someone more... important."

"No one's more important than you, Andi. I'd be lost without you." It was a relief to say something honest, even if he meant it in a business sense, rather than a romantic one.

"I guess I should get the fancy one. If they're going to talk, let's give them something to talk about."

"That's the attitude." Jake rang the bell on the counter and the jeweler appeared again like Rumpelstiltskin. "We'll take it."

The old man beamed. "An excellent choice. I wish you both a lifetime of happiness."

Me, too, thought Jake. He'd need to think on his feet when Andi snapped out of this thing.

Four

Andi blinked as they stepped out of the dark shop into bright morning sunlight that reflected off everything from the gray cobbles to the white-crested mountain peaks that loomed over the town. The cold air whipped at her skin and she drew her warm coat about her. Out in the open she felt violently self-conscious about the huge ring on her finger, and gratefully tucked it into her coat pocket.

"The coffeehouse is just up the road." Jake took her arm. "You may not remember, but they have the best hot chocolate in the known world and you love it."

Andi's muscles tightened at the reminder that he knew more about her than she did. "Do you go there often?" It seemed odd for a king to frequent a local café. Then again she had no idea what was normal. Very strange how she remembered things like old fairy tales but not her own life.

"Of course. Got to support the local businesses."

He certainly was thoughtful. That cozy feeling of being protected and cared for warmed her as he slid his arm through hers again. How lucky she was! No doubt her memory would come back soon and—

A moped skidded past them on the narrow street. Its rider, a man in a black leather jacket, stopped and leaped off, camera in hand. "Your Highness, is it true you are engaged?" he asked, in a French accent.

Jake paused. "It is true." Andi stared in surprise at his polite demeanor.

"May I take your picture?"

Jake took Andi's hands in his. "What do you say, Andi? He's just doing his job."

Andi cringed inwardly. She didn't want anyone seeing her in her confused state, let alone photographing her. She also didn't want to make a fuss in front of a stranger. That might give the game away.

She swallowed. "Okay, I guess." She pushed a lock of hair self-consciously off her face. She hadn't had time to style it—not that she even remembered what style she usually wore—but Jake had assured her it looked lovely.

The man took about fifty pictures from different angles through a long, scary-looking lens that would probably show every pore on her face. Jake was obviously used to the attention and remained calm and pleasant. He even adjusted them into several dignified romantic poses as if they were at a professional shoot.

Almost as if he'd planned this encounter.

She fought the urge to frown, which certainly wouldn't be a good idea for the pictures. How did the photographer know they were engaged when it had only happened last night?

Jake managed to politely disengage them from the impromptu photo session and continue down the road.

He smiled and nodded at passersby, all of whom seemed quite comfortable rubbing shoulders with their monarch. But when they reached the main square she saw two more reporters, a woman with a tiny microphone clipped to her jacket and a tall man with a notepad. They greeted Jake with warm smiles and asked if congratulations were in order.

Andi tried to maintain a pleasant expression while unease gnawed at her gut.

"How does it feel to marry a king?" asked the woman, in soft Ruthenian tones.

"I'm not sure yet," admitted Andi. "Since we're not married. I'll have to let you know after the ceremony."

"When will that be?" asked the man. Andi glanced at Jake.

"We'll make an announcement when we have all the details sorted out. A royal wedding isn't something you rush into."

"Of course." The reporter was a middle-aged woman with soft blond hair. "And you've kept your promise of choosing your bride before Ruthenia's third Independence Day next week."

"The people of Ruthenia know I'm a man of my word."

Andi only just managed not to frown. He'd become engaged to her at the last minute because of some promise he made? That was awfully convenient. The knot in the pit of her stomach tightened.

The woman asked if she could see Andi's ring. Andi pulled it out and was alarmed to see it looked even bigger and brighter out here in daylight. The camera flashed several times before she could hide her hand back in her pocket again.

When Jake finally excused them, her heart was pounding and her face flushed. She let out a silent sigh of relief as he guided her into the warm and inviting coffee shop. She removed her coat and hung it on a row of iron hooks that looked hundreds of years old.

"I'm glad they didn't ask any questions I couldn't answer."

"The paparazzi are polite here." Jake took her hand and led her to a secluded table. "They know I can have them clapped in irons if they're not."

She glanced up to see if he was kidding and was relieved to see a sparkle of humor in his eye.

"The press has been helpful in letting the world know about my efforts to bring the country into the twenty-first century. It pays to keep them happy."

"How could they know about our engagement already? Did that girl you spoke to phone them?" Andi sat in the plush upholstered chair. A small fire snapped and sizzled nearby. The coffee shop had dark wood paneling and varied antique tables and chairs clustered around the low-ceilinged space that looked unchanged since the 1720s—which it probably was.

"I doubt it. They seem to know everything. It's a bit spooky at first, but you get used to it. Maybe they saw us inside the jeweler's?"

"Or maybe he tipped them off." Andi gingerly pulled her be-ringed hand from her pocket to take a menu from the elegantly attired waiter.

"Old Gregor is the soul of discretion." Jake studied his menu. Andi wondered for a second how he knew to trust Old Gregor. Had he commissioned gems for other women? But he said they'd been dating for years.

She cursed the hot little flame of jealousy that had flickered to life inside her. Why were they suddenly engaged after years of dating? Was it somehow precipitated by this promise he'd made, or had she previously refused?

For a moment Andi was hyperaware of people at tables all around them, sipping their drinks and eating. Could they tell she was missing a huge part of her life?

He shrugged. "It's their job. We live in the public eye." He reached across the table and took her hand. His strong fingers closed around hers. She squeezed his hand back and enjoyed the sense of reassurance she got from him. "You'll get used to it again."

"I suppose I will." She glanced warily about the interior of the intimate coffeehouse. "It's so unnerving not to even know what's normal. Then you can't figure out what's odd and unusual."

"It would certainly be odd for us to sit here without drinking hot chocolate." He summoned the waiter and ordered a pot of hot chocolate and a dish of cream. "And, just so you know, the waffles with summer berries are your favorite."

"Did we eat here together a lot?" The place didn't look especially familiar.

"Yes. We often brought business associates and visitors from the States here, since it's so quaint and unchanged. Now that we're engaged..." He stroked her hand inside his and fixed his dark eyes on hers. "It's just the two of us."

Andi's insides fluttered as his gaze crept right under her skin. If only she could remember what their relationship was like. It didn't sound as if they ate out unless in company, which was a bit odd. A secret affair.

It must be strange and unsettling for him to have her behaving like a different person.

Then again, he didn't seem rattled by the situation. His handsome face had an expression of calm contentment. The chiseled features were steady as the mountains outside and it was hard to imagine him getting upset or bothered by anything. Jake was obviously the kind of man who took things in stride. Her hand felt totally comfortable in his, as if he was promising her that he'd take care of her and make sure only good things happened.

Why did it feel so bizarre that such a gorgeous and successful man was all hers?

Well, of course she had to share him with a small nation, but after the lights went out he was hers alone. Hope and excitement rose through her, along with a curl of desire that matched the steam rising off the hot chocolate.

Jake kept his gaze on her face as the waiter poured the fragrant liquid into two wide round cups and then dropped a dollop of thick whipped cream on top of each one. When the waiter moved away, Jake lifted her hand to his lips and kissed it. Sensual excitement flashed through her body at the soft touch of his mouth on her skin, a promise of what would come when they were alone together.

Andi fought the urge to glance around to see if anyone had witnessed the intimate moment. She drew in a deep breath and forced herself to display the kind of cool that Jake possessed naturally. She'd better get used to being in the public eye, since she'd be spending the rest of her life in it.

If she really was marrying Jake. The idea still seemed too far-fetched and outrageous to truly believe. He gently let go of her hand and she moved it quickly to her cup and covered her confusion with a sip. The rich and delicious chocolate slid down her throat and heated her insides. Perfect.

Everything was perfect. Too perfect.

So why couldn't she escape the niggling feeling that when she got her memory back she'd discover something was horribly wrong?

Andi grew increasingly nervous as they drove back to the palace. None of the other staff knew about their engagement—at least as far as she knew. How would they react?

She climbed out of the car on shaky legs. Did she have a best friend here in whom she confided? Or was that person Jake? Tears hovered very close to the surface, but she tried hard to put on a brave face as they approached the grand doorway up a flight of wide steps.

"Good morning, sir." A black-attired man opened the door before they even reached it. "And may I offer you congratulations."

Andi cringed. They all knew already? Word spread around this tiny country like a plague.

"Congratulations, Andi. I'm not sure whether it's appropriate to tell you that, as usual, the mail is in your office."

She didn't even know she had an office, let alone where it was. She gulped, realizing that she'd be expected to do her job, regardless of whether or not she could remember how.

Either that or tell everyone that her mind had been wiped blank, and she couldn't face that. "Thanks," she managed.

She kept her hand buried deep in the pocket of her wool coat as they crossed the marble-floored entrance hall. Faces looked vaguely familiar, but she couldn't remember names or if they were friends as well as coworkers. Jake stopped to answer some questions about a phone call they'd received, and Andi hesitated, unsure which direction to walk in, or where to even hang her coat. Worse yet, a girl with lots of red hair rushed up to her, wide-eyed. "Why am I the last to know everything?"

Andi managed a casual shrug.

The redhead leaned in and lowered her voice. "I see you decided not to leave after all?"

Andi's eyes widened. "Leave?" She glanced up to see if

Jake had heard, but he was still deep in conversation several yards away.

"Stop acting innocent. I saw the suitcases you bought in town. Still, obviously something better than a new job came up."

"I don't know what you're talking about." Truer words were never spoken. Anxiety churned the hot chocolate in her stomach. Suitcases? A new job? That was odd. She needed to get to her room and see if she could find something to jog her memory.

If only she knew where her room was.

She remembered the way back to Jake's suite, and was tempted to head that way without him just to get away from the inquisitive redhead. Then again, he was apparently her boss, so that might look odd.

The ring practically burned her finger, still hidden deep inside her coat. "Let me take that for you." An older man with neat white hair crossed the floor. Andi stared. "Your coat," he continued, demonstrating the hanger in his hand. "I wonder if it's premature to call you Your Majesty?" he asked with a kind expression.

"Probably." She managed a smile while shrugging the coat off. She looked up at Jake and their eyes met. He must have seen the plea in her face as he detached himself from his questioner and strode to her side. "Let's head for my office."

As soon as they were on the stairs, she whispered that she didn't know where her room was. He frowned for a second, then smiled. "We'll go there right now."

The hallway was empty. "I don't even know anyone's name. It's the most awkward feeling. People must think I'm so rude."

"That was Walter. Worked here back when it was a hotel

and always the first to know every bit of gossip. He probably spread the word."

"This building was a hotel?"

"For a while. It had a few different lives while my family was in exile in the States. It took a lot of work to get it looking like this, and you were in charge of most of it."

Andi bit her lip, walking along carpet she may even have selected. Jake pointed to the third polished wood door in a long hallway, only a few yards from his. "That's yours. It wasn't locked when I came to get your clothes."

She tried the handle and it swung open. A neat, hotel-like room greeted her, with heavy brocade curtains and a small double bed. The dark wood furniture looked antique and impressive. She cringed at the sight of a pair of panty hose draped over the bed.

"Um, maybe I should spend a little time alone here. See if anything jogs my memory."

"Sure." Jake stroked her back softly. Her skin heated under her T-shirt as he turned her toward him and lowered his face to hers. All worries and fears drifted way for a few seconds as she lost herself in his soft and gentle kiss.

"Don't worry about anything." He pointed to a dresser. "Your phone's right there and you've always told me I'm programmed in as number one." He winked. "I'll head for my office to deal with this electrical supply situation that's cropped up. Call me if you need anything, and even if you don't."

Her fingers felt cold as he released them from his, but she couldn't help a sigh of relief as she closed the door behind him and found herself alone in the room. At last she could... fall apart.

Part of her wanted to run to the bed and collapse on it, sobbing. But another, apparently more influential, part wanted to pull open the drawers and search for signs of who she was. She tucked the stray panty hose back into their drawer, wondering if she'd taken them out when she was dressing in her evening gown. She wasn't wearing any when she'd woken up in the morning.

The drawer was rather disorganized, as if everything was just shoved in there without much thought. What did this tell her about herself? She frowned and pulled open the drawer above it. Three carelessly folded blouses and some socks gave no further encouragement about her organizational skills.

The closet door was slightly ajar and she pulled it open. An array of colorful suits hung from the hangers, along with several solid-colored dresses and skirts. At least it didn't look as messy as her drawers. She pushed some hangers apart and pulled down one of the suits. A medium blue, it was tailored but otherwise quite plain. She tried to smooth out a horizontal crease that ran just below the lapels. Another crease across the skirt made her frown. Why would a suit hanging in a closet have creases running across it?

She pulled out another suit and saw that it too had lines running through the middle. A forest-green dress also showed signs of having been folded recently, and a navy skirt and... She stopped and frowned. All the items in the closet had crease marks running across them. Not deep, sharp creases, but soft ones, as if they'd been folded only for a short time. What could that mean?

After she hung the suit back in the closet, she walked into the attached bathroom. A floral smell hovered in the air and felt reassuringly familiar. Her favorite scent? She recognized it—which meant it was a memory. Cheered, she examined the cosmetics arranged on a low shelf. There were a lot of lipsticks. She pulled one open and applied it. A rather garish orangey-pink that didn't do her complexion any favors. She put it back on the shelf and wiped her lips with a tissue.

She found the bottle of scent and removed the cap. Warmth suffused her as she sprayed some on her wrists and inhaled the familiar smell. Relief also swept through her that at least something around here felt familiar.

The scent...and Jake.

Excitement mixed with apprehension tickled her insides. How odd that they'd become engaged and she'd lost her memory in the same night. She couldn't help wondering if the two things were related.

Jake was lovely, though. He'd been so sweet and encouraging with her since she'd lost her memory. She was lucky to be engaged to such a kind and capable man. A bit odd that he was a king, but that was just one facet of him. Just a job, really. No doubt she wasn't bothered by his royal status or she wouldn't have become romantically involved with him in the first place.

She picked up her hand and looked at her big diamond ring. It was beautiful and fit her perfectly. She'd feel comfortable wearing it once she got used to it.

Once she got used to any of this.

A knock on the door made her jump. "It's me, Livia."

Andi gulped. Apparently she was supposed to know who Livia was. So far no one seemed to know about her memory except Jake and the doctor, but that was bound to change unless it came back soon. She smoothed her hair and went to open the door.

It was the same red-haired girl from downstairs. The one who'd talked about her leaving. She had a huge grin on her freckled face. "You are a dark horse."

Andi shrugged casually, as if admitting it, even though she didn't know exactly whether Livia referred to the engagement or her memory loss.

"You never breathed a word. How long have the two of you been…?" Her conspiratorial whisper sounded deafening in the quiet hallway.

"Come in." Andi ushered her into the room. Livia glanced around. Andi got the idea that she hadn't been here before, so they probably weren't the closest of friends, but maybe she could learn something from her. She managed a smile. "We didn't really want anyone to know. Not until we were sure."

Livia seemed satisfied with that answer. "How romantic. And after working together all these years. I never suspected a thing!"

"I hardly believe it myself."

"So the suitcases were for your honeymoon." Livia grinned and shook her head. "Where are you going?"

"Not sure yet." Jake hadn't said anything about a honeymoon. Surely they had to have a wedding first.

"This time make sure I'm not the last person in the palace to know. I know you're always insisting that it's part of your job to keep mum about things, but I can't believe I had to learn about your engagement on the radio."

"What did they say?"

"That you and Jake were out ring shopping in town this morning, and you told reporters you were getting married. Hey, let's see the rock!" She reached out and grabbed Andi's hand. "Wow. That's some ring. I wouldn't go on the New York City subway in that."

So Livia had come from New York, as well? That meant they'd probably known each other at least three years. Andi felt awful that she didn't even remember her.

Livia sighed. "And just imagine what your wedding dress will be like. You could probably get anyone in the world to design it for you. Some people have all the luck."

Andi was sorely tempted to point out that she had the

bad luck to not even know who she was, but a gut instinct told her not to confide in Livia. She sensed an undercurrent of jealousy or resentment that made her reluctant to trust her.

"Oh, there are the suitcases, under your bed." Livia pointed. Andi could see the edges of two black rolling cases.

"You're very obsessed with those."

"I thought you were going to take off and leave us. At least to do that interview."

Andi frowned. Had she planned a job interview somewhere?

"I was even starting to think that if we both went back to New York we could share an apartment or something. Guess I was wrong." She widened her eyes, which fell again to Andi's hand.

"You were. I'll be staying here." She smiled, and conviction filled her voice. How nice it was to be sure of something.

"I bet you will."

A million questions bounced around Andi's brain, as many about Jake and life at the palace as about herself. But she couldn't think of any way to ask them without giving the game away, and she wasn't ready to do that yet. On the other hand, at least Livia could help her find her way to her own office. That would be one less problem for her to bother Jake with.

"Why don't you walk to my office with me?"

Livia looked curious. Andi worried that she'd made a misstep. She had no idea what Livia did at the palace, and her clothing, dark pants and a blue long-sleeved peasant shirt, didn't offer any clues. "Sure."

They set out, Andi lagging a fraction behind so that Livia could lead the way without realizing it. They went along the hallway in the opposite direction from Jake's suite, and up a flight of stairs to the third floor. At the top of the stairs a blond man hurried up to them. "Goodness, Andi. Congratulations."

"Thanks." She blushed, mostly because she had no idea who he was. Luckily it was an appropriate response.

"Cook wanted me to ask you whether we should do duck or goose on Thursday for the Finnish ambassador."

"Whichever she prefers would be fine." She froze for an agonizing second while it occurred to her that Cook might be a he.

His eyes widened. "I'll let her know. I suspect you have a lot on your plate right now, what with, well, you know." He smiled. "We're all very happy for you, Andi."

She forced another smile. He'd looked surprised by her lack of decisiveness. She must usually be a very take-charge person. At least the engagement gave her an excuse to be out to lunch—literally and figuratively. She was "preoccupied."

They reached a door halfway down a corridor on the third floor, and Livia hesitated. Andi swallowed, then reached out a hand and tried the door. The handle turned but didn't open it. "Oh no. I forgot my key! You go on with what you're doing and I'll go back and get it. See you later."

Livia waved a cheery goodbye and Andi heaved a sigh. She counted the doors along the hallway so she could find her way here alone next time. Back in her room she searched high and low for the key. When she found a black handbag at the bottom of her closet, her heart leapt.

She'd already discovered that the phone in her bedroom was for business only. Not a single personal number was stored in it. She'd called each one with hope in her heart, only to find herself talking to another bank or supplier. She must have another phone somewhere.

Eager to see her wallet and find out some more about herself, she dove into the bag with her hands. A neat, small wallet contained very few clues. A New York driver's license, with an 81st Street address, about to expire. A Ruthenian driver's license ornamented with a crest featuring two large birds. A Visa credit card from an American bank, and a MasterCard from a European one.

She seemed to be living a double life—half American and half Ruthenian. But that wasn't unusual among expats. She probably kept her accounts open, figuring she'd go back sooner or later.

The bag did contain a keychain containing two keys—her bedroom and office? Other than that there was a small packet of tissues and two lipsticks. No phone. Disappointment dripped through her. Maybe she just had no life.

Except Jake.

She glanced at the business phone on the dresser and her nerves sizzled with anticipation at the thought of calling him. She felt a lot safer in his large, calm presence.

But she didn't want to be a bother. She'd wait until she really needed him.

Keys and phone in the pocket of her jeans, she set off back for the locked office. Her instincts proved correct and the smaller key opened the door. Like her bedroom, her office was neat and featureless, no photos or mementos on the desk. She'd be worried that she was the world's dullest person, except that apparently she was intriguing enough for a king to want to marry her.

She opened a silver laptop on the desk. Surely this would reveal a wealth of new information about her life—her work, anyway. But the first screen asked her to enter her password.

Andi growled with frustration. She felt like she was looking for the password to her own life and it was always just out of reach. Password, password. She racked her brain for familiar words. *Blue,* she typed in. The screen was blue. Nothing happened. *Jake?* Nothing doing. *Love?*

Nada. Apparently her computer, like her memory, was off-limits for now.

Irritation crackled through her veins. She pulled open the drawers in the antique desk and was disappointed to find nothing but a dull collection of pens, paper clips, empty notebooks. The entire office revealed nothing about her. Almost as if every trace of her individuality had been stripped away.

The way you might do if you were leaving a job.

A pang of alarm flashed through her at the thought. Had she stripped her office bare in preparation for abandoning it? She could see how getting engaged to Jake could mean her leaving her job as his assistant, or at least changing it dramatically. But surely Jake would have mentioned it?

She picked up her phone and punched in his number. Feelings of helplessness and anxiety rose inside her as she heard it ring, but she fought them back.

"Hi, Andi. How are you doing?"

A smile rose to her lips at the sound of his deep, resonant voice. "Confused," she admitted. "I'm in my office and feeling more lost than ever."

"I'll meet you there."

She blew out a long breath as she put the phone back in her pocket. It was embarrassing to feel lost without Jake at her side, but wonderful that she could call him to it at any moment. She glanced at the ring on her finger. The big diamond sparkled in the sunlight, casting little shards of light over her skin, a symbol of his lifelong commitment to her.

At least she knew what it felt like to be loved.

She flew to the door at the sound of a knock. A huge smile spread over her face at the sight of him, tall and gorgeous, with a twinkle in his dark eyes.

"I missed you," he murmured, voice low and seductive.

"Come in." Her belly sizzled with arousal and her nipples tightened just at the sight of him. "Do you always knock on my office door?" It seemed oddly formal if they'd worked together and dated for years.

A shadow of hesitation crossed his face for a split second. "I suppose I do. Would you prefer me to barge right in?"

"I don't know." She giggled. Nothing seemed to matter all that much now that Jake was here. "I guess it depends on if I'm trying to keep secrets from you."

"Are you?" His brow arched.

"I have no idea." She laughed again. "Hopefully if I do, they're not very dark ones."

"Dark secrets sound rather intriguing." He moved toward her and lifted his hand to cup her cheek. Her skin heated under his palm. "I might have fun uncovering them."

Their lips met, hot and fast, and his tongue in her mouth drove all thoughts away. She pressed herself against him and felt his arms close around her. *Much better.* Wrapping herself up in Jake was the best medicine for anything that ailed her.

His suit hid the hard muscle beneath it, but that didn't stop her fingers from exploring his broad back and enjoying the thickness of his toned biceps. Her fingertips were creeping into his waistband when a sharp knock on the door made them jump apart.

She blushed. "Do we get carried away like that often?"

Jake shot her a crooked smile. "Why not?"

A glance at the door sent her cheer scattering. "I won't recognize the person."

"I'll help you out."

She drew in a deep breath as she approached the door. "Who is it?"

"Domino." A male voice. "Just wanted to take a peek at Jake's calendar for tomorrow."

She glanced back at Jake and whispered, "I have no idea where your calendar is."

"You can peek at it in my head, Dom." Jake's voice boomed across the room.

A compact, dark-haired man in a gray suit flung the door open and entered. "Sorry, Mr. Mondragon, I didn't know you were in here. I just wondered if there was a set time for the Malaysian High Commission's arrival."

Andi listened while Jake rattled off a few planned events for the following day and tried to keep them filed in her brain in case anyone else asked her. It couldn't hurt to practice using her memory again. Still, she didn't truly breathe again until Domino backed out with a slight bow.

"I feel like the world's most incompetent assistant. Is the calendar on the computer?"

"Yup."

"It's password protected and I don't know the password. Do you know it?"

Jake looked thoughtful. "No."

"Any ideas what it might be?"

"None whatsoever. I guess there are some dark secrets between us." He lifted a brow playfully. "Maybe you have it written down somewhere."

"That's another thing." She frowned, apprehension twisting her gut as she prepared to tell him. "There's nothing personal in here at all. It's all business all the time, as if all the personal effects had been removed."

Jake blinked and his gaze swept the room. A furrow deepened between his brows; then he shrugged. "I'm not much for personal knickknacks in the office, either. Why don't we take a break and go stroll around the palace? Then at least you'll know where everything is."

Andi was a bit alarmed by the brusque way he changed the subject. One question burned in her mind. "Am I still your assistant? I mean, now that we're engaged."

"Yes, of course." Jake looked startled for a second. "I'd be lost without you arranging my life."

"Then prepare to get lost, since I can't arrange my own computer desktop right now." Tears loomed again. Apparently they'd never been very far away. "I still don't remember anything at all."

Jake took her into his arms again. His scent, familiar and enticing, wrapped around her as his embrace gave her strength. "The doctor said it would take time for your memory to return. Come on, let's go for that walk. There's no point getting upset over something you can't control."

The palace was so large that probably no one knew exactly how many rooms it had or how to get to all of them. As Jake explained, it had been the home of several dynasties of Ruthenian royals, all of whom had left their own stylistic stamp, so the building had everything from fortified turrets to elegant rows of French windows opening out onto a terrace for alfresco dancing.

As they walked about, on the pretext of discussing the decor, everyone stopped to offer their congratulations on their engagement. Some people hid their surprise, but Andi could tell it was a startling occurrence. Could they really have not noticed a romance occurring—over several years—right beneath their noses?

Five

"Jake, congratulations on your engagement." The silvery tones emerging from his phone dripped with acid. Jake glanced across his suite to where Andi reclined on the sofa looking through a tourist brochure about Ruthenia.

"Thanks, Carina." Lucky thing she couldn't see how happy he was not to be marrying her.

"Quite a surprise." Her tone was cool. "I had no idea you were involved with your assistant."

"You know how these things are. It seemed...unprofessional, but you can't halt the course of true love." He'd already explained the same to three other would-be queens, so it rolled naturally off his tongue.

"Indeed." She cleared her throat. "Daddy accuses you of toying with my affections, but I assured him that I'm a big girl and that he should still fund the new industrial development."

These veiled threats were becoming familiar, too.

"I do hope he will. We look forward to entertaining you both at the palace again soon." He was smiling when he hung up the phone. Right now everything was going as smoothly as could be expected. He was now officially off the hook for choosing the next queen of Ruthenia. No one had actually pulled support from any key projects or threatened to fund a revolution. It was probably a plus that he hadn't offended one Ruthenian big shot by choosing the daughter of another. Selecting his American assistant as his bride had left all the local families equally offended—or mollified. And so far things were working out nicely.

He couldn't understand why he'd never plotted this tidy solution together with Andi, before she lost her memory. Choosing his wife now seemed like an agenda item he'd neatly checked off.

"Why don't you join me on the sofa?" Her come-hither stare and soft tones beckoned to him.

Blood rushed to his nether regions and he stiffened. Of course there were some aspects of their engagement that should remain off-limits until Andi's memory came back. It was one thing to pretend to love your assistant, it was quite another thing to actually make love to her.

"That dinner was delicious, but I find I'm still hungry." Andi's blue eyes sparkled. She curled her legs under her and stretched one arm sensually along the top of sofa.

Her voice called to a part of him that wasn't at all practical. Jake was struck by a cruel vision of the black lacy underwear beneath her jeans and T-shirt. *She'll be angry if you sleep with her under false pretenses.*

But were they really false? He did intend to marry her.

Which was funny, as he'd never planned to marry anyone. His parents' long and arduous union—all duty and no joy— had put him off the whole institution from an early age. They'd married because they were a "suitable" match, his father the son of the exiled monarch and his mother the daughter of a prominent noble, also in exile. They'd soon discovered they had nothing in common but blue Ruthenian blood, yet they'd held up the charade for five decades in the hope they'd one day inhabit this palace and put the Ruthenian crest on their stationery again.

They were both gone by the time the "new regime" crumbled and Ruthenia decided it wanted its monarchy back. Jake had assumed the mantle of political duty, but it didn't seem fair or reasonable to expect him to take it into his bedroom, as well.

He'd much rather take Andi into his bedroom. Her lips looked so inviting in that sensual half smile. And he could just imagine how those long legs would feel wrapped around his waist....

But that was a really bad idea. When she got her memory back she'd likely be pretty steamed about the whole scenario he'd cooked up. She'd be downright furious if he took advantage of her affections, as well. Much better if they kept their hands to themselves until they could talk things over sensibly.

"Do you want me to walk you back to your room?" His voice sounded tight.

"Why? I'm not going to sleep there, am I?" She raised a brow. She seemed far more relaxed, bolder, than he'd seen her so far. She was obviously feeling comfortable, even if her memory still showed no signs of returning.

"I think you should. It's a question of propriety."

She giggled. "You are joking."

"No." He felt a bit offended. "It's a royal thing."

"So, we've never...?" She rose from the sofa in an athletic leap and strode across the room. "I don't remember the details about my own life, but I remember general stuff and I'm pretty sure that it's totally normal for dating couples to…sleep together. So I don't believe that we've been dating for years and never done more than kiss."

Jake shrugged. She had a point. If only she knew he was trying to protect her. "Okay, I admit we may have been… intimate. But now that we're engaged and it's all official and formal, I think we should play by the rules."

"Whose rules?" She raised her hand and stroked his cheek with her fingers.

His groin tightened and he cleared his throat. "Those official, hundreds-of-years-old rules that the king should keep his hands off his future bride until after the wedding."

Her mouth lifted into a wicked smile. "These hands?" She picked up his hands and placed them squarely on her hips. Heat rose in his blood as he took in the curves beneath his palms. She wriggled her hips slightly, sending shock waves of desire pulsing through him.

I'm in full control of my hands and my mind. The thought did nothing to reassure him, especially when one of his hands started to wander toward her backside. Andi pressed her lips to his and her familiar scent filled his senses. Next thing he knew his hands were straying up and down her back, enjoying the soft curves under his palms.

His pants grew tight as Andi pressed her chest against his. He could just imagine what those deliciously firm breasts must look like in her lacy bra. If he coaxed her out of her T-shirt—which would not be difficult—he could find out right away.

But that might lead to other things.

In fact, he was one hundred percent sure that it would.

He pulled back from the kiss with considerable effort. "Don't you have some…embroidery to do or something?"

"Embroidery?" Laughter sparkled in her clear blue eyes. "Do I really embroider stuff?"

He chuckled. "Not that I know of, but does a man really know what his fiancée gets up to in the privacy of her room?"

"I guess that depends how much time he spends there." She raised a brow. "Maybe we should go to my room?"

Jake froze. That seemed like a really bad idea. Which underlined what a bad idea all this kissing and cuddling was. Much better to keep things professional, with just enough hint of romance to keep the people around them convinced. At least until Andi came back to her senses.

He flinched as Andi's fingers crept beneath the waistband of his pants. He'd grown rock hard and the thought of pushing her away was downright painful. Her soft cheek nuzzled against his and his fingers wandered into her hair. She looked so different with her hair loose, much less formal and more inviting.

Her cool fingers slid under his shirt and skated up his spine. Jake arched into the sensation, pulling her tighter into his embrace. Her breathing was faster and her pink lips flushed and parted. He couldn't resist sticking his tongue into her mouth and she responded in kind, until they were kissing hard and fast again.

"Still think I should go to my room?" She rasped the question when they came up for air.

"Definitely not." He had to take this woman to bed, whether it was a good idea or not.

He reached under her T-shirt and cupped her breast, enjoying the sensation of skin and scratchy lace under his fingers. He could feel her heartbeat pounding, like his own, as anticipation built toward boiling point.

"Let's go into the bedroom." He disentangled himself from her with some effort and led her into the other room. The plain white bedcovers looked like an enticing

playground and he couldn't wait to spread her out on them
and uncover her step by step.

He swept her off her feet—eliciting a shriek of delight—
and laid her gently on the bed.

Suddenly horizontal, Andi looked up at Jake with alarm.
Her entire body pulsed and tingled with sensation. About
to reach for the buttons of his shirt, her fingers stopped in
midair. Their eyes met, his dark with fierce desire that made
her insides tremble.

Everything about this situation felt new and different.

Jake's hands showed no hesitation as he unzipped
her jeans and slid them off. Heat snapped in her veins,
deepening the sense of unease creeping over her.

"What's the matter?" Jake paused and studied her face.

"I don't know. It just feels strange."

"Go with it." He lifted the hem of her T-shirt and eased
it off over her head. Her nipples stood to attention inside
her lacy bra, which was now exposed to view along with
its matching panties. Jake's devouring gaze raked her body
and Andi felt both very desirable and very, very nervous.

Jake unbuttoned his own shirt and shrugged it off,
revealing a thickly muscled chest with a line of dark hair
running down to his belt buckle. His powerful biceps flexed
as he undid the belt and the button of his pants.

Andi's hesitation flew away. "Wait, let me do that."
She rose to the edge of the bed and unzipped his pants
as excitement and arousal replaced her apprehension. She
pushed them down to reveal dark boxers and powerful hair-
roughened thighs.

Both in their underwear, they stretched out on the cool
white sheets, skin to skin. She touched his chest with a
tentative finger, enjoying the warmth of his body. She
traced the curve of his pec and traveled lower, to where his

arousal was dramatically evident against the dark fabric of his shorts.

Jake's taut belly contracted as she trailed over it then paused.

She looked up at his face. The naked desire in his eyes further unraveled her inhibitions. She let her hands roam lower, tugging at his boxers until they slid down and his erection sprang free. She gasped, and he chuckled. Then she pulled the soft fabric down over his strong legs until he was totally naked.

"You're gorgeous," she breathed. Then she blushed, realizing that must sound silly when she'd seen him naked many times before.

"You're far more gorgeous." His slightly callused fingers tickled her skin as he ran his hand along her side, from her bra to her panties.

"But you're not seeing me as if it was the first time."

"Yes, I am," he murmured. Then he looked up. "At least that's what it feels like." Excitement danced in his dark eyes. "I could never grow tired of looking at you."

Andi swallowed. If Jake's feelings for her were anything like the intense roar of passion pulsing in her veins right now, she could understand how this could feel new and fresh even after several years.

He slid his arm behind her back and tugged her closer. Her belly flipped as it touched his, and her breasts bumped against his chest.

"Time to unwrap this present," he breathed. He propped himself on one elbow and deftly undid the clasp on her bra, releasing her breasts. She felt his breathing quicken as he tugged the lacy fabric off over her arms and lowered his mouth to one tight pink nipple.

Andi arched her back and let out a little moan as Jake flicked his tongue over the delicate skin. The sound of her own voice in the still night air startled her, and quickened her pulse further. She pushed her fingers into his thick hair and enjoyed the silky sensations roaming through her body as he licked and sucked.

"Kiss me," she begged, when she couldn't take the almost painful pleasure anymore. He responded by pressing his lips to hers with passion and kissing the last of her breath away.

Arms wrapped around him, she held Jake close. His warm masculine scent filled her senses and the heat of his skin against hers only increased her desire. Fingers trembling with anticipation, she took hold of his erection. Jake released a low moan as she ran her fingers over the hard surface, then tightened them around the shaft, enjoying the throb of pleasure that issued through him.

Had she really done this before? She couldn't believe it. Again that odd sensation of unfamiliarity almost dampened her pleasure. Everything she did was like taking a step into the dark and hoping the floor would still be there under her foot when she put it down. Where would these strange and intense sensations and urges lead her?

Jake's mouth crushed over hers once more and her doubts crumbled beneath the fierce desire to feel him inside her.

Working together they eased off her pantics and he climbed over her. The inviting weight of him pressed against her chest for a moment; then he lifted himself up with his powerful arms and entered her slowly.

Too slowly.

She found herself writhing and arching to encourage him deeper. Her insides ached to hold him and her whole body burned hot and anxious with an urgent need to join with him. Her fingers dug into his back as he finally sank all the way in and she released a deep moan of pleasure into his ear.

Jake layered hot kisses along her neck and cheek as he moved over her, drawing her deeper into the mysterious ocean of pleasure that felt so strange and so good at the same time. They rolled on the bed, exploring each other from different angles and deepening the connection between them. Her hands wandered over his body, enjoying the hard muscle, squeezing and stroking him as he moved inside her.

She loved riding on top of him, changing the rhythm from slow to fast and back again as the sensations inside her built toward a dangerous crescendo. Jake was over her again when she felt herself suddenly lose control of her muscles and even her mind as a huge wave of release swept her far out of herself. She drifted in limbo as pulses of sheer pleasure rose through her again and again. Then she seemed to wash back up in Jake's arms, exhausted and utterly at peace.

"That was…" She couldn't seem to find the words. Any words, really.

"Awesome."

Jake's unroyal response made her laugh. "Exactly." Then she frowned. "Is it always like this when we…make love?"

She could swear she felt him flinch slightly. "Yup. It is."

"I guess that's good." She smiled. She must be one of the luckiest people on earth, to have a loving relationship—with really hot sex—with this ridiculously handsome man who just happened to be a king.

She stretched, still feeling delicious pulses of pleasure tickling her insides. She couldn't help wondering how she'd arrived at this juncture. How did she find herself engaged to a gorgeous monarch? Maybe she was from some kind of upper-crust family herself. It was so odd not knowing anything about yourself. She opened her eyes and peered at Jake.

"Will you tell me some things about myself?"

His sleepy gaze grew wider and a smile tilted his mouth. "Like what?"

"My background, the kind of things I like to do, that sort of stuff."

He frowned, still smiling that half smile. "Hmm, it's hard to know where to start."

Adrenaline buzzed through her at the prospect of nailing down a few details. "How about at the beginning. Did I grow up in New York?"

"No. You moved there after college." He kissed her cheek softly. "You came to work for me right after you graduated."

"What did I study in college?"

"Hmm. I can't remember exactly. I think it was something to do with literature. Or maybe French. You spoke French fluently even though you'd never been to France. I remember that."

"Oh." It wasn't so odd that he didn't know what she'd majored in. That was before she met him. "Where did I go to college?"

Jake hesitated, and frowned. "Was it U Penn? Somewhere in Pennsylvania. I'm pretty sure of that."

"You don't remember where I went to college? You're almost as bad as I am. Where did I grow up?"

Jake licked his lips. His eyes showed a mild trace of alarm. "Pennsylvania, definitely. Philly, maybe. Or was it Pittsburgh?"

"We've never been there together?" An odd knot of tension was forming in her stomach. She propped herself up in bed on one elbow.

"No, our relationship has always been pretty under wraps. The whole professional thing."

"So you haven't met my family." Again, unease niggled somewhere deep inside her.

"No. You have parents and a sister somewhere, though. You get together with them for holidays."

"In Pennsylvania?"

"I think so. You usually took the train."

"Oh." How odd that she couldn't remember anything about them. Or Pennsylvania. And it was a little disturbing that Jake seemed to know so little about her. Did they never talk about her past? "What's my sister's name?"

Jake pursed his lips for a moment. "I don't know."

"I guess I didn't talk about her that much." Maybe she and her sister weren't close. What a shame. Maybe she'd try to improve their relationship once she got her memory back. "What about my parents? Do you know their names or where they live? We could get in touch with them and see if they could jog my memory back into existence."

Jake's brow had furrowed. "I suppose we should be able to find that information somewhere."

"It's probably on my computer if I could just figure out the password."

"We'll worry about that in the morning." Jake pulled her closer to him. "Right now let's just enjoy each other."

Andi let out a sigh and sank back into his arms. "You're right. Why get stressed out over something I can't control?"

But even in his soothing embrace, there wasn't a single second when she didn't ache to recover her memory—and her history. How could you really go forward, or even live in the moment, if you don't know who you are?

After breakfast, Jake left Andi in her office to look over her files. She seemed anxious that she wasn't able to do her job since she didn't remember the details of palace life, let alone any specific events. He mused that he should have been concerned, too, since a key purpose of this whole engagement was to keep her at his side running the show, but somehow the palace was managing to tick along. And he was enjoying her company far more than he'd imagined.

How could he have worked with her for six years and not even know where her family lived? As far as he knew she was born behind the desk in his Manhattan office. And he cringed at not knowing her sister's name. For all he could remember she just referred to her as "my sister."

He strode to his current office, intent on mining it for the information he should know simply on the basis of their long acquaintance. They spent all day together—did they usually talk about nothing but work?

Andi was always excellent about keeping them focused so no time was wasted. She managed their affairs with such efficiency that there was little downtime for chin-wagging, especially since they'd moved to Ruthenia and tackled challenges higher than the legendary Althaus mountains that loomed over the palace. He'd always appreciated her professional approach to her job and to life in general.

But now he was beginning to realize he'd missed out on enjoying her company all this time. She was much more complex than he'd realized, more vulnerable and intriguing—and not just because of her missing memory. He'd never seen her as a person with emotions, with needs, before, because she'd done such an excellent job hiding that aspect of herself.

And he'd never realized she was so tempting. She'd hidden that, too.

He closed his office door and walked through to the cabinets in the file room, where the personnel files from New York were stored. Thanks to Andi's relentless organization he quickly laid his hands on her file, and the résumé she'd submitted when she applied for the job as his admin back when he was simply a venture capitalist.

A quick scan revealed that she'd graduated from Drexel University in Pennsylvania—right state, at least—with a degree in business administration and a ridiculously long list of clubs and activities to her name. Apart from some temping in Manhattan, her first job was with him. She'd graduated from North Hills Senior High School in Pittsburgh—ha, right again, maybe he wasn't so bad after all. He had to congratulate himself on being able to pick such a promising employee despite her lack of relevant work experience.

But that didn't solve his current problem of finding out about her past and helping her recover her memory.

Wait. Did he even want her to recover her memory? If she did, she'd surely remember that their relationship had been strictly professional and the whole engagement his invention.

Discomfort rose in his chest, threatening to overwhelm the sense of satisfaction—of happiness, dammit—that had suffused his body and mind since their overnight encounter.

Andi was sensational between the sheets. He'd never have dreamed that his quiet, prim assistant hid so much passion and energy beneath her suited exterior. She even looked different, like she'd forgotten to put on the mask of no-nonsense propriety she usually painted on with makeup and pinned into place with a spritz of hair spray. The real Andi—the one without the mask—was soft and sexy and downright irresistible.

Desire stirred inside him again, tightening his muscles. Blood rushed to his groin as he thought about her in his arms that morning, scented with passion as well as her usual floral fragrance. He put the résumé back in its file.

Maybe her memory wouldn't come back and they could start over from the night he'd found her dancing outside, freed of the inhibitions and anxieties built by a lifetime of experience. He couldn't help believing that the woman who'd shared his bed was the real Andi, and that she'd been hiding inside all this time, waiting for a chance to be free.

Andi let out a cry of sheer joy. She'd finally cracked the password on her computer. A cryptic penciled list in the drawer seemed like a meaningless string of words—until she started typing them in one by one.

Queen had proved to be the key that unlocked her hard drive, and possibly her whole life. Funny! She must have picked it because she knew she soon would be queen.

That thought stopped her cold for a second. Queen Andi. Didn't quite sound right. Still, she'd get used to it. And maybe Andi was short for a more majestic name, like Andromeda or something.

Her heart raced as the computer opened her account and laid a screen full of icons out before her. Yikes. So many different files, some with the names of countries, some of companies. She didn't know where to start. A sound issued from the machine, and she noticed that the email icon announced the presence of fifty-three messages. She clicked on it with a growing sense of anticipation, and scrolled back to the last one she had opened. Eticket confirmation.

Frowning, she opened the email, which revealed an itinerary for Andi Louise Blake—apparently she wasn't really named Andromeda—to travel from Munich to New York. The date listed was…yesterday.

Her blood slowed in her veins and her breathing grew shallow.

Obviously she hadn't gone on the trip, and if it was a business-related one, surely Jake would have mentioned it.

Munich—the nearest international airport, perhaps?—to New York, where she used to live...

She had been planning to leave.

Head spinning, she sat back in her chair. Why would she leave, if she was in love and about to get engaged?

She should just ask Jake about this. Why get all worked up when it could be a business trip that just got canceled at the last moment, maybe due to her loss of memory, or their engagement?

Andi glanced down at her ring with a growing sense of unease. She never had figured out why her clothes were creased as if they'd been packed. She must have changed her mind and unpacked at some point, but when? And why did Jake not know about her plans to take off?

Had she issued an ultimatum and forced him into proposing to her?

She swallowed, then started to chew on a nail. Her stomach curled up into a tight ball. Maybe she should see what else was going on in her email before she spoke to Jake.

It was hard to read with so much nervous energy leaping through her system. Her eyes kept jumping around on the screen. Most of the emails were business related—responses to invitations, scheduling questions, orders for supplies and that kind of thing.

Then one titled What's going on? from a Lizzie Blake caught her eye. Blake—the same last name as her. What *was* going on? She clicked on it with her heart in her mouth.

Andi, I know you told me not to email personal stuff to this account, but I've tried calling you and you won't call back. We saw a news story on TV yesterday saying that you're going to marry Jake Mondragon, your boss. Is this true? How come you didn't tell us? I thought you were getting ready to quit from the way you've been talking lately. Mom is pretty upset that you'd keep something like this from us. I remember you saying years ago that your boss was hot, but you never mentioned dating him, let alone getting engaged. Anyway, get in touch ASAP and let me know if I need to find a dress for a royal wedding. XX Sis.

Andi sat back, blinking. She had a sister called Lizzie. Who knew absolutely nothing about her relationship to Jake. And who'd been calling her but not getting through. She *must* have another phone somewhere that she used for personal calls.

She scanned the rest of the emails, but nothing else looked truly personal.

Where would she keep another phone? Brain ticking fast, she hurried back to her bedroom, glad she didn't run into anyone in the hallway—especially Jake.

A pang of guilt and hurt stung her heart. She was avoiding him. Only this morning they'd lain in each others arms and she'd enjoyed such contentment and bliss that she hadn't even minded about her memory being gone.

Now she was racked with suspicion and doubt. She locked her bedroom door behind her and started to go through the closet and drawers again. Finally, in the pocket of a black pair of pants she found a small silver phone. The pants showed signs of being recently worn—slightly creased across the hips and behind the knees—so maybe she had them on just before she lost her memory.

She flipped the phone open and pulled up recent messages. There were three from Lizzie and one from her mom, who sounded noticeably upset. Her voice, with its hint of tears, struck a sharp and painful chord deep inside her. On instinct Andi hit the button to dial the number.

"Andi!"

"Mom?" Her voice shook slightly. "Is it really you?"

"Of course it's me. Who else would be answering my phone?" A bright laugh rang in her ear. "What the heck is going on over there?"

Andi drew in a steadying breath. "I don't really know, to be honest. I lost my memory."

"What?"

"Jake found me dancing around outside and I couldn't remember anything at all. I didn't even remember you or Lizzie until I saw her email and found the messages on my phone."

"Oh, my gosh, that sounds terrifying. Are you okay?"

"More or less. It's been strange and kind of scary, but I'm not sick or injured or anything."

"That's a blessing. Has your memory come back?"

Andi blinked. A blurry vision of a face—an energetic woman with short light brown hair and bright blue eyes filled her brain. "I think it's coming back right now. Do you have blue eyes?"

"Of course I do. That's where you got them from. You forgot my eye color?"

"I forgot you even existed. I didn't know my own name." Other images suddenly crowded her brain: a man with gray hair and a warm smile, a blonde with long curls and a loud laugh. "But it's coming back now that I hear your voice." Excitement crackled through her veins. Finally she had an identity, a past. The details crashed back into her brain one after the other—her childhood home, her school, her old dog Timmy...

"Are you really engaged to your boss?" Her mom's voice tugged her back to the present.

Andi froze. That part she didn't remember. "He says we got engaged right before I lost my memory. I don't remember it."

"Do you love him?" The voice on the phone was suddenly sharp.

"Oh, yes. I've always loved him." The conviction rang through her whole body. "I've loved him for years."

"You never said a thing. I had no idea you were even involved with him."

Andi blinked rapidly. The memories flooding her brain were curiously devoid of any romantic images of her and Jake. She had plenty of memories of working with him, but as she mentally flipped through them looking for signs of their relationship a strange and awful truth dawned on her. "That's because I wasn't involved with him."

Six

Her mom's confused and anxious reaction prompted Andi to make excuses and hang up the phone. She needed someone who could answer questions, not just ask them. Instinct told her to call her sister, Lizzie.

"Your Majesty!" Her sister's now-familiar voice made her jump.

"Lizzie, you wouldn't believe what's been going on."

"You're right. I don't, so you'll have to break it down into tiny pieces for me. Are you really marrying your boss?"

Andi bit her lip. "I don't know. It's the weirdest thing, I lost my memory and ever since then we've been engaged. But my memory's coming back now—since I found your phone messages and spoke to Mom—and I don't remember anything at all about being engaged to him."

"You never even told me you were dating him."

"I don't remember anything about that, either. I do recall being seriously attracted to him for, oh, years and years, but not that anything actually came of it. Now suddenly I seem to be engaged to him and I have no idea what's going on."

"How does he explain the situation?"

Andi blew out. "I don't know. I haven't spoken to him about it yet. My memory only just started coming back and he doesn't know yet."

"Do you remember him asking you to marry him?"

She thought for a second. "No. I don't remember everything, though. There's a gap." She raised a hand to her head where she could still feel a slight bump. "I must have fallen and banged my head, or something." She paused, remembering the etickets she'd seen on her computer. "Did I say anything about coming back to the States?"

"For Christmas, you mean?"

Andi wondered how much to reveal, then decided things were so complicated already that she might as well be truthful. "For good. I think I was planning to leave here. I had tickets back to New York."

"And you don't remember why?"

I do.

The realization was seeping back into her, almost like blood rushing to her brain. She had intended to leave. She wanted to go because she was tired of adoring Jake while he flirted with other women in the name of business.

Because she loved him and knew she could never have him.

A sharp pain rose in her middle around the area of her heart. How had six years of yearning turned—overnight—into a fantasy engagement?

It didn't add up. There was a missing piece to the puzzle and she had no idea what it was.

"So are you marrying him, or what?" Lizzie's amused voice roused her from her panicked thoughts.

Her eyes fell on the big ring, flashing in the afternoon

sunlight pouring through the large office window. "Yes." Then she frowned. "At least I think so."

"Well, I saw it in the *National Enquirer,* so it must be true, right?" Lizzie's voice was bright with laughter. "There's a picture of you with a rock on your finger the size of my Mini Cooper. Is that thing real?"

Andi stared at the glittering stones. She was pretty sure it was a real diamond, but was it a real engagement ring? "Sure. It's from a jeweler here in town. Jake bought it for me yesterday."

"Sounds pretty official to me. Is he good in bed?"

Andi's mouth fell open.

"Come on, I'd tell you. Or do royal romances not involve any sex?"

Her teasing voice brought a smile to Andi's lips. "He's amazing."

"Ha. I had a feeling. I've seen pictures of him and he's seriously handsome. I love the dark flashing eyes. Is he romantic?"

"Very." She could almost feel his arms around her right now, holding and steadying her. "He's been so sweet with me since I lost my memory. We've managed to keep it a secret so far. You and Mom and the doctor he called are the only other people who know."

"Why keep it a secret?"

"I guess because I felt so vulnerable. Like everyone around me knows more about me than I do. I didn't want anyone to know. It's all coming back now, though. Not all the tiny details yet, like work stuff I have to do, but the bigger things like who I know and where I'm from and…"

How much I've always loved Jake.

Were they really going to be married and live happily ever after? It seemed too much to hope for.

"So you're going to be a queen. Will I have to curtsy to you?"

"Gosh, I hope not." Andi laughed. "What a strange idea. I can't quite see myself with a crown on."

"You'd better get used to the idea. Can I be your maid of honor? Or maybe they don't have them in Ruthenia."

"I have no idea. I've never planned a wedding here and apparently I haven't paid close enough attention at the few I've attended." Images of Jake's other would-be brides crowded her mind. Alia and Maxi and Carlotta and Liesel... there were so many of them. Rich and beautiful and fawning all over him. Why, out of all the glamorous and powerful women available to him, had Jake chosen her?

It was time to track him down and ask some questions.

After promising to call Lizzie back and tell her the details, Andi went into the bathroom and looked in the mirror. Her cosmetics were strung out along a shelf, which was not how she used to keep them. She also remembered that she nearly always tied her rather wispy hair up in a bun and slicked it down with gel—she was always experimenting with different brands as the Ruthenian climate was surprisingly humid. Now her hair lay loose around her shoulders, and her face looked oddly colorless without the lipstick and blush she usually donned.

A glance in her closet reminded her she was a hard-core suit wearer. She felt it was important to project a professional image, and she liked bright colors as they seemed assertive and positive. Right now she had on a rather uncharacteristic pastel yellow blouse and a pair of slacks and her hair wafted around her shoulders. People must have noticed the difference.

Part of her felt embarrassed that she'd been walking around the palace looking like a paler, less polished version of herself. And part of her wondered whether Jake actually preferred the less made-up look. He'd chosen the super-casual jeans and T-shirt she'd worn all the previous day. She blushed as she remembered he'd also chosen the racy lingerie. A glance in her underwear drawer confirmed that cotton briefs and no-nonsense bras were more her style.

Still, if Jake liked lacy lingerie and jeans, she could adjust. She couldn't resist smoothing just a hint of blush on her cheeks. They were a bit pale with shock. But she used a clear gloss instead of lipstick and left her hair loose—maybe it didn't look so bad after all.

With a deep breath, she set off for his office. Her pulse rate roared like a runaway truck by the time she finally plucked up the courage to peek around the open door. Jake was in conversation with a man she instantly remembered as the minister of economics. Jake looked up when she entered the doorway, and an expression flickered across his face—shock?—almost as if he suddenly knew her memory was back.

Andi struggled not to fidget as the conversation continued for another couple of minutes—something urgent to do with trade tariffs. Her nerves were jumping and her palms sweating.

In his dark suit, with his usual air of unhurried calm, Jake seemed perfectly poised and in control of any situation. She, on the other hand, had no idea what their situation really was. She could remember nearly everything about her life—except a romance with Jake.

He finally closed the door behind the economics minister and turned to her. Again she could see in his face that he knew something was different.

"My memory is coming back." She floated the words out, as if on a string, wondering what his response would be. Would he take her in his arms with a cry of joy?

Jake didn't move an inch. "That's great." He seemed to be waiting for her to reveal more.

"It started when I saw an email from my sister. Then I phoned my mom. That jogged something in my brain and the memories started bubbling up."

"What a relief." His voice was oddly flat. He still made no move toward her.

Andi's eyes dropped to her ring, which seemed to sting the skin underneath it. "It's strange, I remember working with you for years, but I don't..." Her voice cracked as fear rose in her chest. "I don't remember anything about us." She faltered. "I mean us being...romantically involved."

Jake stepped up to her and took her hand. Her heart surged with relief and she was about to smile, but his deadly serious demeanor stopped her. "I'll be completely honest with you."

"About what?" Her pulse picked up and a sense of dread swelled inside her.

"We weren't involved. Our relationship was strictly professional until two days ago."

"We weren't dating? Not even in secret?" Her heart hammered against her ribs.

"No."

Andi swallowed hard and her rib cage tightened around her chest. The ostentatious ring suddenly seemed to weigh down her hand and drain her strength. "So, the engagement is fake?" Her voice came out as a rasping whisper, filled with every ounce of apprehension and terror she felt. "It was all pretend?"

Jake tilted his head. "No."

Andi wanted to shake him. "Could you be more explicit?"

He frowned. "It's hard to explain. You were going to leave, and I didn't want you to. I was under pressure to choose a bride, and then you lost your memory. Things fell into place and I realized you're the ideal woman to be my wife."

She blinked, trying to make sense of his words. "So we are engaged?"

"Absolutely." His dark eyes looked earnest.

Then a cold sensation crept over her. "But you're not in love with me."

He swallowed. "Love is something that grows over time. I'm confident that we'll enjoy a happy and successful marriage. The important thing is to provide stability for Ruthenia, and as a team we can do just that."

Andi struggled for breath. The man of her dreams, whom she'd fantasized about and mooned over for six long years, wanted to marry her.

Because she'd be a key member of his team.

A cold laugh flew from her lips. "Wouldn't it have been easier to just offer me a higher salary?"

He raised a brow. "I tried that."

"And I said no? Wait. Now I remember saying no. You were so sure you could talk me around, just like you always do." Her vision blurred as tears rose to her eyes. "And you really thought I'd go along with this crazy plan?"

"You're sensible and practical. I knew you'd see the sense in it."

"In spending my life with a husband who doesn't love me? You never even noticed I was female." A flashback to their lovemaking filled her brain. He'd noticed it then. But maybe he'd just pretended she was one of the glamorous socialites that usually buzzed around him. He'd had no shortage of girlfriends in the time she'd worked for him.

"My parents married because their families were both exiled Ruthenian nobles. They were married nearly fifty years."

His parents had died before she met him. She knew little about them except that they were part of New York society. "Were they happy?"

He hesitated. "Of course."

"You don't sound convinced. Did they love each other?"

"It was a successful marriage, and they achieved their lifelong goal of producing an heir who'd be ready to take the throne of Ruthenia when the time came."

"Lucky thing you were cooperative. It would be a shame to throw away fifty years of your life and have your son insist he was going to be a pro skateboarder. Did you really think I'd just go along with your plan?"

"Yes."

His calm expression exasperated her. He still thought she was going to go along with his scheme. He obviously didn't care about her feelings at all. "We slept together." Her body still sizzled and hummed with sensual energy from that amazing night.

The passion they'd shared might have been fake on his side, but on hers it was painfully real.

"I didn't intend for that to happen." His expression turned grim. "I understand that you must be furious with me for taking advantage of your situation."

"You're right. I am." Devastated would have been a better word. Their lovemaking wasn't the fruit of a long-term and loving romance, at least not for him. On her side she'd probably had enough romance in her head to last a lifetime.

He must have found it hilarious that she fell into his arms so easily. "Didn't you think it was wrong to sleep with an employee?"

His eyes narrowed. "Yes. I didn't intend to sleep with you until I'd explained the situation."

"Until you'd explained to me that you needed a wife and I was handy?" She still couldn't quite believe he took her so totally for granted.

Obviously he had no respect for her feelings and wishes. A chill swept through her and she hugged herself.

"You were confused after losing your memory. I didn't want to complicate matters when I knew you were in no state to make an important decision."

"So you just made it for me."

He drew in a breath. "You know me well enough to trust my judgment."

She struggled to check her anger. "I trust your judgment perfectly in matters of business, but not where my personal life is concerned. You already knew I intended to leave because I wasn't feeling fulfilled."

No need to say she couldn't stand to see him marry another woman. He'd assume she was thrilled that he'd made a coldhearted and clinical decision to marry her. "It's downright arrogant of you to assume I'd marry you."

"I know you're capable of rising to any challenge."

"But what if I don't want to?" Her voice rose a little and she struggled to check tears. A romance with Jake was such a heartfelt wish. Suddenly it had become a duty.

No doubt sex with her was supposed to seal the pact in some way.

What a shame she'd enjoyed it so much. Right now she wanted to chastise her body for still craving his touch. She should hate him for what he'd done when she needed his help the most.

Jake still stood there, calm and regal, chin lifted high.

A sinister thought crept over her. If he could plan something so outrageous as marriage to a woman who didn't know who she was, perhaps he contrived to put her in such a vulnerable position.

"Were you responsible for me losing my memory?" If he'd gone this far in his deception, who knew what he could be capable of?

"No." His answer was decisive.

She wanted to believe him—and hated herself for it.

"Then what did happen?" So many pieces were still missing.

"I don't know how you lost your memory. I found you outside dancing around on the grass in the moonlight."

Andi blushed. Had she done anything embarrassing? She couldn't remember a single thing about that night. Though now that he mentioned it, she did remember telling him she was going to leave. A cold sensation slithered through her. She was leaving to protect her heart.

Right now her heart was being flayed open. Jake's desire to keep her had nothing to do with him wanting her as his fiancée, or even his friend, and everything to do with keeping his office running smoothly.

And he'd seduced her into his bed on the pretext that they'd been dating for years.

Her insides still hummed with sense memories that would probably torment her forever. She'd thought they were making love—and her whole spirit had soared with the joy of it—but he was just cementing a deal.

On instinct she pulled the big ring from her finger. It wedged a bit over the knuckle, but she managed to get it off. "Take this back."

His eyes widened. "Oh, no. You must wear it."

"I don't have to do anything." She shoved it forward. "It's not real."

"I assure you those stones are genuine and worth a large sum of money."

Andi's mouth fell open, then closed shut. How could he not understand a word she was saying? She walked to his desk and put the ring down on the polished surface. It looked odd there, sparkling away amongst the piles of papers.

"I don't intend to wear or own any kind of engagement ring unless I'm actually engaged. And since we're not really engaged or even involved, I don't want anything to do with it." Tears threatened in her voice. She crossed her arms, and hoped it would hide the way her hands were shaking.

"But we are engaged." Jake's words, spoken softly, crept into her brain and heart. "I really do want to marry you."

Andi blinked, trying to catch her breath. How could a dream come true in such a horrible, distorted way?

The odd expression in his eyes almost made her consider it. There was something like…yearning in their dark depths.

Then again, she was obviously good at dreaming stuff up.

Now that her memory was back she knew—in the depths of her aching soul—that she'd loved Jake for years, pined for him and hoped that one day he'd see her as something other than an efficient assistant. She'd adored him in silence, occasionally allowing herself to fantasize that things might one day be different if she waited patiently for him to notice her. Their time as an engaged couple was the fulfillment of all secret hopes—and now she'd woken to find herself living a mockery of her cherished dreams.

Anger flared inside her, hot and ugly. "You honestly think I would continue with this charade that you sprung on me when I was at my most vulnerable? To let people think that we love each other when we're nothing more than boss and assistant, as always?"

"We'll be equals, of course, like any couple."

He said it simply, like he really believed it. But then Jake could convince anyone of anything. She'd watched him in action for too long. "I'm not sure that many couples are equals, especially royal ones." She'd be the official wife, sensibly dressed and courteous as always. The one who got left behind with her embroidery—not that she did embroidery—while he was out having affairs with other women.

"I need to leave, and right now." If she continued with this pretense for even another hour, she'd get sucked into hoping their official engagement might turn into true romance. Even with every shred of evidence pointing to that being impossible and hopeless, she'd already proven herself to be that kind of softheaded, dreaming fool.

"The story's gone around the world already."

She steadied herself with a breath. All her relatives knew, probably all her old friends. Everyone she'd ever known, maybe. "You'll just have to explain that it was all a big lie. Or a joke." Her voice cracked on the last word. It did feel like a cruel joke at her expense. She'd never experienced such feelings of happiness and contentment as during the last couple of days as Jake's fiancée. Their night of lovemaking had raised the bar of pure bliss so high that she'd likely never know anything like that again.

"I'm going to pack my bags." She turned for the door. Her whole body was shaking.

Jake caught hold of her arm and she tried to wrench it away, but his grip was too strong. "The people of Ruthenia are counting on you. I'm counting on you."

His words pierced her soul for a second, but she summoned her strength. "I'm sure the people of Ruthenia can find something else to count on. Television game shows, perhaps."

"We're going to be on television tonight. To talk about celebrating our engagement during the Independence Day celebrations."

Andi froze. "Independence Day. That's what this is all about, isn't it?" She turned and stared at his face. A memory of Jake's public promise to choose a wife formed in her mind. "You committed to picking a bride before Ruthenia's third Independence Day." She squinted at him, looking for signs of emotion in his face. "Your deadline had come right up on you and you had to pick someone or you'd be a liar. And there I was, clueless as a newborn babe and ripe for duping."

"Andi, we've been partners for years. It's not that big a leap."

"From the office to a lifetime commitment? I think that's a leap. You can't just get a plane ticket and leave a marriage." She lifted her chin as anger and hurt flashed over her. "Though apparently I can't just get a plane ticket and leave my job with you, either." Fury bubbled up inside her. "Do you think you can control everything and everyone?"

"I'm not trying to control you, just to make you see sense. We're a great team."

"I've never been into team sports. When I marry, it will be for love." Her heart ached at the thought that she'd loved Jake almost since the day she met him.

Though right now she hated him for tricking her into a relationship that meant nothing to him.

"Think it over, Andi. Be sensible."

"I am sensible. That's why I know this would never work."

Jake's expression grew impenetrable. "Stay until after Independence Day, at least."

"You think I'll change my mind? Or maybe you think I'll just be guilt-tripped into marrying you by seeing all those smiling Ruthenian faces. What if people don't like the idea of you marrying your lowly assistant? They'd probably rather see you marry some Ruthenian blue blood with twelve names."

"They'll all know I made the right choice."

His words hung in the air. *The right choice.*

Impossible.

Still, his quiet conviction both irked and intrigued her.

She stared hard at his chiseled face. "You really do want to marry me?"

He took her hands in his. Her skin tingled and sizzled, and she cursed the instant effect he always had on her. "I do want to marry you."

Those accursed hopes and dreams flared up inside her like embers under a breath.

He doesn't love you. Don't get carried away.

Still, maybe something could come of this crazy situation. Could she live with herself if she didn't at least try to make it work?

She inhaled a shaky breath. "If I agree to stay until Independence Day, then decide it won't work, you'll let me go?"

His expression clouded. "Yes."

She wasn't sure she believed him. Jake didn't often admit, or experience, defeat. But she could always sneak away this time.

Or stay here for the rest of her life.

Her heart thumped and her stomach felt queasy. "I can't really believe this is happening. We'll sleep in separate rooms?"

"If you prefer." His cool reply sounded like a challenge. He probably intended to seduce her again. She silently determined not to let him.

"Independence Day is three days away." Could she stand to be Jake's unloved but practical fiancée for seventy-two hours? She really didn't want to let everyone down and ruin the Independence Day celebrations. She could look at it as her job, as long as there was no kissing or sex involved.

And then there was that insane hope that they really could live happily ever after.

Jake picked up the ring from among the papers on his desk. "You'll need this."

Andi eyed it suspiciously. Putting the ring back on would mean agreeing to his terms. Clearly he expected her to, and why wouldn't he? She'd always done everything he asked in the past.

He picked up her hand without asking permission. Her skin heated instantly at his touch and she made the mistake of looking up into his face. His dark gaze dared her to refuse him—and she knew in that instant that she couldn't.

Why did he still have so much power over her?

She was disoriented right now. Confused. Her memory slipping and sliding back into her head while she tried to take in the strange new reality of Jake wanting to marry her.

Wanting to *marry* her.

It should be a dream come true—so why did it feel more like a waking nightmare?

Seven

The following afternoon, Andi adjusted the collar of her new and fabulously expensive dress. Fit for a queen. The rack of designer clothes had arrived with a coordinator from Ruthenia's most snooty bespoke tailor to help her choose the right look and make any necessary alterations.

She'd tried not to tremble when the seamstress stuck pins in around her waist and bust. Now the freshly sewn green fabric draped over her like a second skin of luxurious silk.

But did she look like a future queen? She'd be paraded on TV as one tonight. RTV was setting up cameras in the ballroom to interview her and Jake. She'd tried to beg off and delay any public appearances until after she'd made her decision, but endless calls from the television station had hounded her into it and at this point she'd appear snooty and uncooperative if she said no again.

"Earrings." A representative from the jeweler where

they'd bought the ring opened a case filled with sparkly gems. Andi hadn't even noticed her come in, but then people were coming and going in a constant scurry, preparing for the evening shoot. The earrings blurred into a big shiny mass.

"You choose." Andi didn't even want to look at them. Better to let these professionals decide whether she looked like a future queen or not.

She certainly didn't feel like one.

Was it her job to act this part? It felt more like her patriotic duty. Which was silly since she was American, not Ruthenian. At least until she married Jake.

If she married Jake.

She tried to keep her breathing steady as the girl clipped big emeralds to her ears and murmured, "Perfect." The seamstress nodded her approval and beckoned across the room.

A middle-aged woman with a blond pompadour and a rat-tail comb approached with a gleam in her eye. She picked up a strand of Andi's limp hair between her thumb and finger and winced slightly. "Don't worry. We can fix it."

Thirty minutes later her hair hung around her shoulders in plump curls that everyone assured her looked "lovely." The woman staring back at her from the mirror, wide-eyed and pale beneath her carefully applied makeup, didn't even look like her. She'd barely managed to remember who she was, and now she was being turned into someone else.

"Andi, can you come in for a moment? They want to check the lighting."

She steadied herself and walked—slowly in her long, rather heavy dress—toward the formal library where the cameras were set up.

Jake was nowhere to be seen.

It's your job, she told herself. Just be professional. Being a monarch's fiancée definitely felt more like a career assignment than a romantic dream come true.

Strangers' hands shuffled her into place under blistering hot lights that made her blink. More powder was dotted on her nose and fingers fluffed her curls. Out of the corner of her eye she could see the local news anchor going over some notes with a producer. What kind of questions would they ask?

I won't lie.

She promised herself that. This whole situation was so confusing already; she had no intention of making it worse by having to keep track of stories. She'd try to be tactful and diplomatic, of course.

Just part of the job.

A sudden hush fell over the room and all eyes turned to the door. His majesty. Jake strode in, a calm smile on his face. Andi's heartbeat quickened under her designer gown. Fear as well as the familiar desire. Would she manage to act the role of fiancée well enough to please him?

She cursed herself for wanting to make him happy. He hadn't given her feelings any thought when he'd tricked her into wearing his ring.

Their eyes met and a jolt of energy surged through her. *I really do want to marry you.* His words echoed in her brain, tormenting and enticing. How could she not at least give it a shot?

A producer settled them both on the ornate gilt-edged sofa under the lights, in full view of three cameras. Andi felt Jake's hand close around hers, his skin warm. She almost wished he wouldn't touch her, as she didn't want him to know she was shaking and that her palms were sweating.

No aspect of her job had ever made her so terrified. She'd greeted foreign dignitaries and handled major international incidents without so much as a raised pulse. Why did every move she made now feel like a matter of life and death?

Silence descended as the interviewer moved toward them, microphone clipped to her blue suit. Andi's heart pounded.

I won't lie.

But Jake didn't have to know that.

"Your Majesty, thank you so much for agreeing to this interview." Jake murmured an assent. "And for allowing us to meet your fiancée." The journalist smiled at Andi.

She tried not to shrink into the sofa. Yesterday morning she'd been totally comfortable and happy as Jake's fiancée. It had felt as natural as breathing. But now everything was different and she'd been dropped into the middle of a movie set—with no script.

The reporter turned her lipsticked smile to Andi. "You're living every young girl's dream."

"Yes," she stammered. *Except in the dream the prince actually loves you.* "I still can't believe it."

No lies told so far.

"Was the proposal very romantic?"

Andi grew hyperconscious of Jake's hand wrapped around hers. She drew in a breath. "I was so stunned I don't remember a word of it."

The reporter laughed, and so did Jake. Andi managed a smile.

"I guess the important part is that you said yes." The reporter turned to Jake. "Perhaps you could tell us about the moment."

Andi stared at Jake. Would he make something up? He'd lied to her when he'd told her they were engaged. Unless a king could become engaged simply by an act of will.

"It was a private moment between myself and Andi." He

turned to look at her. Then continued in a low voice. "I'm very happy that she's agreed to be my wife."

Until Independence Day. He was obviously confident he'd convince her to stay after that, but as she sat here under the lights with people staring at her and analyzing every move she made, she became increasingly sure she'd couldn't handle this.

It would have been different if Jake wanted to marry her for the right reasons and she could look forward to true intimacy and companionship, at least when they were alone together.

But she'd never been enough for him before, and she was painfully sure that she wouldn't be enough for him now—ring or no ring.

"What a lovely ring." Andi's hand flinched slightly under the reporter's gaze. "A fitting symbol for a royal romance."

Yes. All flash and pomp. "Thanks. We bought it right here in town. The local village has such skilled craftspeople."

"I think it's charming that you chose the work of a Ruthenian artisan, when you could so easily have bought something from New York or Paris."

"Both Andi and I are proud of Ruthenia's fine old-world craftsmanship. It's one of the few places where attention to detail is more important than turning a quick profit. Some people might see our steady and deliberate approach to things as a hindrance in the modern world of business, but I see them as strengths that will secure our future."

Andi maintained a tight smile. He was turning their engagement interview into a promotional video for Ruthenia. Something she would have heartily approved of only a few days ago, but now made her heart contract with pain.

With his "steady and deliberate" approach to marriage,

he expected her to devote her life to Ruthenia and fulfill the role of royal wife, whether he loved her or not.

Andi startled when she realized the reporter was staring right at her. She'd obviously just asked a question, but Andi was so caught up in her depressing ruminations that she hadn't even heard it. Jake squeezed her hand and jumped in. "Andi will be making all the wedding arrangements. In our years of working together she's proved that she can pull off the most elaborate and complicated occasions."

He went on to talk about Ruthenian wedding traditions and how they'd be sure to observe and celebrate them.

What about my family traditions? Andi remembered her cousin Lu's wedding two summers ago. A big, fat Greek wedding in every sense of the word. What if she wanted to celebrate her mom's Greek heritage as well as Jake's Ruthenian roots?

Not a chance. Just one more example of how her life would slide into a faded shadow of Jake's.

But only if she let it.

Resolve kicked through her on a surge of adrenaline. She didn't have to do anything she didn't want to. "Of course, we'll also honor our American roots and bring those into our planning. I have ancestors from several different countries and we'll enjoy bringing aspects of that heritage into our wedding."

The reporter's eyes widened. Jake was so big on being all Ruthenian all the time, trying to prove that despite his New York upbringing, every cell in his blue blood was Ruthenian to the nucleus. Right now she couldn't resist knocking that. If he wanted a Ruthenian bride there was no shortage of volunteers.

But he'd chosen an American one. She smiled up at him sweetly. His dark eyes flashed with surprise. "Of course. Andi's right. Our American background and experience have enriched our lives and we'll certainly be welcoming many American friends to the wedding."

Andi felt his arm slide around her shoulders. She tried not to shiver at the feel of his thick muscle through her dress. "And now, if you don't mind, we have a lot to do to prepare for the Independence Day celebrations this week. Our third Independence Day marks a turning point for our nation, with our gross national product up and unemployment now at a fifty-year low. We hope everyone will join us in a toast to Ruthenia's future."

He circled his arm around her back, a gesture both protective and possessive. Andi cursed the way it stirred sensation in her belly and emotion in her heart. The reporter frowned slightly at being summarily dismissed, but made some polite goodbye noises and shook their hands.

Andi let out a long, audible sigh once the cameras finally turned off.

Jake escorted her from the room, and it wasn't until they were in the corridor outside that he loosened his grip on her arm slightly. "Nice point about our American heritage."

She wasn't sure if he was kidding or not. "I thought so." She smiled. "I'm kind of surprised you decided to pick an American wife. I was sure you'd marry a Ruthenian so you could have some ultra-Ruthenian heirs."

An odd expression crossed his face for a second. Had he forgotten about the whole royal heir thing? This engagement scenario seemed rather by-the-seat-of-the-pants; maybe he didn't think it through enough. Did he really want a Heinz 57 American girl from Pittsburgh to be the mother of Ruthenia's future king?

"Being Ruthenian is more a state of mind than a DNA trait." He kept his arm around her shoulders as they marched along the hall.

"Kind of like being king?" She arched a brow. "Though I

suppose that does require the right DNA or there'd be other claimants. The only way most Ruthenians can claim the throne is by marrying you. I guess I should be honored."

Jake turned to stare at her. She never usually talked back to him. Of course she didn't—he was her boss. Maybe once he discovered the real, off-hours Andi had a bit more spunk to her he'd lose all interest in hoisting her up onto his royal pedestal.

"I don't expect you to be honored." Humor sparkled in Jake's dark eyes. Did nothing rile him? "Just to think about the advantages of the situation."

"The glorious future of Ruthenia," she quipped.

"Exactly."

"What if I miss Philly cheesesteak?"

"The cook can prepare some."

"No way. She's from San Francisco. She'd put bean sprouts in it."

"We'll import it."

"It'd go cold on the plane."

"We'll fly there to get some."

"Is that fiscally responsible?"

He laughed. "See? You're a woman after my own heart."

"Cold and calculating?" She raised a brow.

"I prefer to think of it as shrewd and pragmatic." He pulled his arm from around her to reach into his pocket and she noticed they were at the door to his suite. She stiffened. She did not want to go in there and wind up in his bed again. Especially if it was the result of some shrewd and pragmatic seduction on his part.

The intimacy they'd shared left her feeling tender and raw. Probably because she'd always loved him and the act of making love only intensified everything she'd already felt. Now that she knew he didn't love her—that it was a mechanical act for him—she couldn't bear to be that close to him again.

"I guess I'll head for my room." She glanced down at her ridiculously over-the-top interview dress. "Am I supposed to give this dress to someone?"

"You're supposed to wear it to the state dinner to-night."

State dinner? She didn't remember planning any dinner. In fact she remembered deliberately not planning anything for the first few days after she intended to leave. "Maybe my memory isn't fully back yet, but I…" It was embarrassing to admit she still wasn't in full control of her faculties.

"Don't worry, you had nothing to do with it. I pulled the whole thing together to butter up all the people cheesed off by our engagement."

"That's a daring use of dairy metaphors."

Jake grinned. "Thanks. I'm a man of many talents."

If only I weren't so vividly aware of that. She sure as heck wished she'd never slept with him. That was going to be very hard to forget.

"So let me guess, all your recently jilted admirers, and their rich and influential daddies, will be gathered around the table in the grand dining room to whisper rude remarks about me." Her stomach clenched at the prospect.

"They'll do no such thing." Jake had entered the suite and obviously expected her to follow. He'd totally ignored her comment about heading for her room. "They wouldn't dare."

That's what you think. Powerful people could afford to be blissfully ignorant about what others thought, since no one would dare say anything to their face. She, on the other hand, was more likely to get a realistic picture of their true feelings since people didn't bother to try to impress a mere assistant.

But would they act differently now they thought she was engaged to Jake?

She glanced down at her perfectly tailored dress. It might be interesting to see how they behaved now the tables were turned and she was the one about to marry a king.

And it would certainly be educational to see how Jake behaved in their midst now that he was officially engaged to her.

"You look stunning." Jake's low voice jolted her from her anxious thoughts. His gaze heated her skin right through the green silk as it raked over her from head to toe, lingering for just a split second longer where the bodice cupped her breasts.

"Thanks. I guess almost anyone can look good when they have a crowd of professionals available to take charge."

"You're very beautiful." His dark eyes met hers. "Without any help from anyone."

Her face heated and she hoped they'd put on enough powder to hide it. Did he mean it or was he just saying that to mollify her? She didn't really believe anything he said anymore.

On the other hand, maybe he'd come to see her in a new light since he started considering her as wife material. She did feel pretty gorgeous under his smoldering stare.

"Flattery will get you everywhere." A sudden vision of herself in his bed—which was less than forty feet away—filled her mind. "Okay, maybe not everywhere. How long do we have until dinner?" She wasn't sure hanging around in his suite was a good idea. It might be better to spend time in more neutral territory.

"About half an hour."

"And who arranged this dinner if I didn't?" Curiosity goaded her to ask the question. The palace seemed to be running pretty well without her input, which should make her feel less guilty about leaving, but it irked her somewhat, too.

"Livia. She's been really helpful the last few days. Really stepped into your shoes."

"Oh." Andi stiffened. Why did it bother her that Livia might be after her job? She was planning to leave it, after all. Still, now that she remembered more of her past, she knew Livia had always felt somewhat competitive toward her, and resentful that Andi was hand in glove with Jake while she did the more routine work like ordering supplies and writing place cards.

She couldn't help wondering if Livia might now be resentful that Jake planned to marry her—talk about the ultimate promotion.

If you were into that sort of thing.

"Champagne?" Jake gestured to a bottle chilling in a silver bucket of ice. He must have had it brought here during the interview.

"No thanks." Better to keep her head. She had a feeling she'd need it. "But you go ahead."

"I couldn't possibly drink alone. And it's a 1907 Heidiseck."

"Are you sure it's not past its sell-by date?"

He chuckled. "It was recovered from a ship that was wrecked on its way to deliver champagne to the Russian Imperial family. It's been brought up from the bottom of the sea and tastes sublime even after decades of being lost."

"Very appropriate, considering the history of Ruthenia."

"That's what the friend who gave it to me thought. Won't you join me in a toast to our future?" His flirtatious glance tickled her insides.

She took a deep breath and tried to remain calm. "Not until I've figured out whether I want us to have a future."

Jake tilted his head. "You're very stubborn all of a sudden."

"That's because we're discussing the rest of my life, not just some seating placements or even a corporate merger."

"I like that about you. A lot of women would jump at the chance to marry me just to be queen."

Or just because you're embarrassingly attractive and shockingly wealthy. She tried to ignore those enticements herself.

Jake lifted a brow. "That doesn't mean much to you, does it?"

"I've never had the slightest desire to be called Your Majesty."

"Me, either." He grinned. "But if I can learn to put up with it, I'm sure you could handle it, too."

"Did you always know you'd be king one day?" She'd wondered this, but never dared ask him.

"My parents talked about it, but I thought they were nuts. I planned to be a king of Wall Street instead."

"And now you're doing both. I bet your parents would be very proud. It's a shame they weren't alive to see you take the throne." She knew they'd died in a small plane accident.

"If they were alive they'd be ruling here themselves, which would have been just fine with me."

"You don't like being king?" She couldn't resist asking.

"I like it fine, but it's a job for life. There's no getting bored and quitting. Sometimes I wonder what I would have done if I'd had more freedom."

"You were brave to take on the responsibility. Not everyone would have, especially with the state Ruthenia was in when you first arrived."

"I do feel a real sense of duty toward Ruthenia. I always

have, it was spooned into me along with my baby food. I couldn't turn my back on Ruthenia for anything."

She didn't feel the same way. In fact she could leave and never look back—couldn't she? She hadn't been raised to smile and wave at people or wear an ermine robe, but she had always felt a strong sense of commitment to her job—and her boss.

Who stood in front of her tall and proud, handsome features picked out by the light of a wall sconce. She admired him for stepping up to the responsibilities of getting Ruthenia back on its feet, and committing himself to help the country and its people for the rest of his life.

She should be touched and honored that he wanted her help in that enterprise, regardless of whether he loved her.

Still, she wasn't made of stone. Something she became vividly aware of when Jake reached for her hand and drew it to his lips. Her skin heated under his mouth and she struggled to keep her breathing steady.

He's just trying to seduce you into going along with his plan. It doesn't mean he really loves you—or even desires you.

Her body responded to him like a flipped switch, but then it always had, even back when he saw her as nothing more than an efficient employee. Heat flared in her belly and her fingertips itched to reach out and touch his skin.

But she'd resisted six long years and she could do it now.

She pulled her hand back with some difficulty. Her skin hummed where his lips had just touched it. A quick glance up was a mistake—his dark eyes fixed on hers with a smoldering expression that took her breath away.

But she knew he was an accomplished actor. You had to be to pull off international diplomacy, especially when it involved placating all the outrageous characters he dealt with in Ruthenia.

"You're very suspicious." His eyes twinkled.

"Of course I am. I woke up from amnesia to find myself engaged to my boss. That kind of thing makes a girl wary."

"You know you can trust me." His steady gaze showed total confidence.

"I thought I could trust you." She raised a brow. "Over the last day I've learned I can't trust you. You used me to your advantage, without consulting me."

His expression darkened. "I couldn't consult with you because you didn't know who you were."

"You could have waited until my memory came back and we could discuss it calmly." *Instead you decided to convince me between the sheets.* He'd undermined all her inhibitions and drawn her into the most intense and powerful intimacy.

Too bad it had worked so well.

"Time was of the essence. Independence Day is coming right up."

"And you couldn't disappoint the people of Ruthenia."

"Exactly. I knew you'd understand."

She did. The people of Ruthenia and his own reputation were far more important than her feelings.

Did he even know she had feelings?

She had three days to put him to the test.

Eight

Andi would have liked to sweep into the dining room and smile confidently at the gathered Ruthenian dignitaries and their snooty daughters, then take her place at the head of the table.

But it didn't work like that.

The toe of her pointed shoe caught in the hem of her dress on her way into the anteroom and she pitched through the doorway headfirst. Jake, walking behind her, flung his arms around her waist and pulled her back onto her feet before she fell on her face into the Aubusson carpet. It was not an auspicious entrance into high society.

Her face heated, especially when she saw the looks of undisguised glee on Maxi's and Alia's faces.

Jake laughed it off and used the occasion to steal a kiss in front of the gathered audience. She was too flustered to attempt resistance, which would have looked rude and strange anyway, since as far as everyone knew they were madly in love.

The kiss only deepened her blush and stirred the mix of arousal and anguish roiling in her gut.

"Congratulations!" A portly older man with medals on his jacket stepped forward and bowed low to Andi. She swallowed. This was the Grand Duke of Machen. He didn't have any marriageable daughters left, so he was one of the few non-hostile entities in the room. He turned to Jake. "We're all thrilled that you've finally chosen a bride to continue the royal line."

The royal line? Andi's muscles tightened. As Jake's wife she'd be expected to produce the future king or queen. Which meant that even if it were a marriage of convenience, there would be some sex involved. She'd already learned that making love with Jake touched something powerful and tender deep inside her. Not something she could do as a matter of routine. Could he really expect that of her? It was different with men. They could turn off their emotions and just enjoy the pure physical sensations.

If only she could do that.

A glance around the room revealed that not everyone was as thrilled as the grand duke. Maxi's father Anton Rivenshnell looked grim—salt-and-pepper brows lowered threateningly over his beady gray eyes. Maxi herself had abandoned her usual winning smile in favor of a less-flattering pout.

"I suppose an American bride seemed a natural choice when you spent your entire life in America," growled Rivenshnell, his dark suit stretched across an ample belly. "Though this is naturally a disappointment for the women of Ruthenia."

Jake seemed to grow about a foot taller, which, considering his already impressive height of six-one, made him a little scary. "Andi has demonstrated her commitment to Ruthenia over the last three years, living and working by my side. She is one of the women of Ruthenia."

Ha. Andi couldn't help loving his spirited defense of her. "I've never been so happy as I am here." The honest truth. She wasn't going to lie. "I've spent every day enjoying the people and the beautiful countryside, and I've come to love Ruthenia as my home."

"And you fell in love with your boss, too." The grand duke's laugh bellowed across the room.

"Yes." She managed a shaky smile. Again, it was the truth—but no need for Jake to know that. As far as he was concerned she was just fulfilling her part of the arrangement.

Andi felt very self-conscious as they were ushered into the dining room by a rather smug Livia. This was the first time she'd attended one of these affairs as a guest, not one of the staff members hovering along the walls ready to serve the diners and tend to Jake's needs. Livia shot her at least three meaningful glances, though she couldn't actually tell what they meant.

At least she managed not to fall on her face on her way to the end of the table, where she was seated far, far away from Jake, probably in between two daddies of rejected girls.

Jake was seated between Alia and Maxi, just as she'd sat him before she lost her memory. Then she'd done it as a joke, to torment him with his two most ardent admirers and hopefully put him off both of them. Now he must have planned it himself, for reasons she could only guess at.

Did he intend to have affairs with each of them now that he was no longer on the hook to make one his queen? Surely quiet little Andi wouldn't object.

The very thought made her seethe. Still, she didn't

remember Jake ever cheating on one of his many girlfriends. On the other hand, he rarely dated the same one for long enough to get the chance. As soon as a girl showed signs of getting serious, he brought an abrupt end to things.

Andi had rather liked that about him. He never continued with a relationship just because it was there. He was often blunt and funny about the reasons he no longer saw a future with a particular girl. And it always gave her fresh hope that one day he'd be hers.

And now he was. At least in theory.

Irritation flickered through her at the sight of Alia brushing his hand with her long, manicured fingers. Jake smiled at the elegant blonde and spoke softly to her before turning to Maxi. The sultry brunette immediately lit up and eased her impressive cleavage toward him. Jealousy raged in Andi's gut and she cursed herself for caring.

"Your parents must be delighted." The gruff voice startled Andi, who realized she was staring.

"Oh, yes." She tried to smile at the white-haired man by her side. Up close she could see he was probably too old to have a jilted daughter, so that was a plus.

Her parents would be happy if she married Jake. At least she imagined so. How would they feel if she refused to marry him?

"Have they visited Ruthenia before?"

"Not yet. But I'm sure they'll love it here."

"I imagine they'll move here." His blue eyes twinkled with…was it warmth or malice?

"They have their own lives back in Pittsburgh, so I don't think they'll be leaving."

"But they must! Their daughter is to be the queen. It would be tragic for a family to endure such separation."

"It's quite common in the U.S. for families to live hundreds or even thousands of miles apart."

"In Ruthenia that would be unthinkable."

"I know." She shrugged. Was he also implying that having such a coldhearted and independent American as their queen was unthinkable? "But they have jobs they enjoy and friends where they live. I'm sure they'll come visit often."

"They've *never* visited you here? How long have you been here?"

"Three years, but it's an expensive trip and…" He was making her feel bad, and she had a feeling that's exactly what he intended. "Have you ever visited the States?" She smiled brightly. Every time she looked up, someone was peeking at her out of the corner of their eye. Including Livia. She was beginning to feel under siege.

Jake shot her a warm glance from the far end of the table. Even from that distance he could make her heart beat faster. He looked totally in his element, relaxed, jovial and quite at home in the lap of luxury, surrounded by Ruthenian nobles.

Whereas she felt like a scullery maid who'd wandered into the ballroom—which wasn't a million miles from the truth. In all her dreams of herself and Jake living happily ever after, they lived happily in a fantasy world of her own creation. While life in the Ruthenian royal palace was definitely someone's fantasy world, it wasn't hers, and Jake was clearly making a terrible mistake if he thought this could work.

Jake beamed with satisfaction as staff poured the coffee. Andi looked radiant at the far end of the table, resplendent in her regal gown and with her hair arranged in shiny curls that fell about her shoulders. Ruthenia's haughty beauties disappeared into the drapery with her around. He'd tried to reassure them that his marriage was a love match and not a deliberate insult to them and their families. He couldn't afford to lose the support of Ruthenia's most powerful businessmen. Noses were definitely bent out of shape, but no one had declared war—yet.

A love match. He'd used the term several times now, though never within earshot of Andi. He couldn't say something so blatantly untrue right in front of her—at least not now that she had her memory back. He knew nothing of love. Raised by a succession of nannies while his parents traveled, he'd been groomed for duty and honor and not for family life and intimate relationships. Love seemed like something that happened in poems but not in real life, and he didn't want to promise anything to Andi that he couldn't deliver.

He was hotly attracted to her and admired all her fine qualities, and that was almost as good. Many people married for love and ended up divorced or miserable. It was much more sensible to go into a lifetime commitment with a clear head and a solid strategy.

Andi seemed concerned about the lack of love between them once her memory returned and she knew they hadn't been involved. His most important task over the next two days was to convince her they were meant to be together, and surely the best way to do that was to woo her back into his bed. The warm affection they'd shared stirred something in his chest. Maybe it wasn't the kind of love that inspired songs and sonnets, but he ached to enjoy it again.

It took some time for the guests to filter out the front door, and he kept half an eye on Andi the whole time in case she should decide to slip away. She looked tense, keeping up her end of every conversation but looking around often as if checking for escape routes. He'd been so busy rebuilding the relationships he'd worked hard to cement in the past three years by dancing with different girls that he hadn't danced with Andi. There was plenty of time for him to catch up with her after the guests left.

He kissed Alia on the cheek and ignored the subtle squeeze she gave his arm. He slapped her father on the back and promised to call him to go over some business details. So far, so good. Now where was Andi? She'd managed to slip away as the Kronstadts made their exit.

Irritation and worry stirred in his gut along with a powerful desire to see her right now. He strode up the stairs from the foyer and intercepted her in the hallway outside her room.

He slid his arms around her waist from behind—just as he'd done when she dove unceremoniously into their company earlier. A smile spread across his mouth at the feel of her soft warm body in his arms, and he couldn't wait to spend the night together.

But she stiffened. "I'm tired, Jake."

"Me, too." He squeezed her gently. "We can sleep in each other's arms."

"I don't think that's a good idea." She unlocked her door and he followed her in, arms still wrapped around her. Her delicious scent filled his senses. He twirled her around until they were face-to-face—and noticed her face looked sad.

"What's going on, Andi? You did a fantastic job this evening."

Her mouth flattened. "We should close the door, for privacy."

"Sure." That was a promising start. He turned and pushed it shut. "Why do you look unhappy?"

"Because I can't do this. I don't fit in here. I feel like an intruder."

"That's ridiculous. You fit in here as well as I do."

"I don't. I felt out of place and people kept going on about me being American. They obviously don't like the idea of you marrying a foreigner."

"Monarchs nearly always marry foreigners. That's how the British royal family ended up being German." He grinned. "They used to import brides from whichever country they needed to curry diplomatic favor with. It's a time-honored tradition."

"I don't think marrying me will get you too far with the White House."

"Oh, I disagree." He stroked her soft cheek with his thumb. "I'm sure any sensible administration would admire you as much as I do."

Her eyes softened for a moment and a tiny flush rose to her pale cheeks. But she wouldn't meet his gaze.

He placed his hands on either side of her waist. She had a lovely figure, a slender hourglass that the dress emphasized in a way her stiff suits never could. The tailored bodice presented her cleavage in a dangerously enticing way, and a single diamond sparkled on a fine chain between her small, plump breasts.

A flame of desire licked through him. "You were the loveliest woman in that room tonight."

"You're sweet." There was no hint of sparkle or a smile in her eyes. She didn't seem to believe him.

"You know I'm not sweet." He lifted a brow. "So you'd better believe me. Every minute I danced with those other girls, I wished I was dancing with you."

But you weren't.

He'd danced with those women because it was good for the nation's economy to keep their families on his side. Maybe he'd desired them, too, but that wasn't why he twirled them around the floor. Andi knew that business would always come first with Jake. She's always known that, and admired it. But now that she contemplated the prospect of spending the rest of her life with a man who didn't love her, it seemed like a mistake.

Mostly because she loved him so much.

The press of his strong fingers around her waist was a cruel torment. Her nipples had thickened against the silk of her bodice, aching for his touch. The skin of her cheek still hummed where he'd brushed his thumb over it.

She even loved him for the fact that he'd marry a woman he didn't love just for the sake of his country. That kind of commitment was impressive.

Unless you were the woman he didn't love, and had to watch from the sidelines, or even under the spotlight, while he gave his heart and soul to Ruthenia and its people.

His presence dominated her room, with its neat, impersonal decor. He was larger than life, bolder, better-looking and more engaging than any man she'd ever met. Wasn't it enough that he wanted to marry her?

Why did she think she was so special she deserved more than he offered? Maybe it was the independent-minded American in her who wanted everything. It wasn't enough to be queen and have a handsome and hardworking husband—she had to have the fairy-tale romance, as well.

Jake leaned in and kissed her softly on the mouth. Her breath caught at the bottom of her lungs as his warm, masculine scent—soap and rich fabrics with a hint of male musk—tormented her senses. Her lips stung with arousal as he pulled back a few inches and hovered there, his dark gaze fixed to hers.

Her fingers wanted to roam under his jacket and explore the muscles of his back and she struggled to keep them still at her sides. If she let him seduce her she was saying "yes" to everything he offered.

Including sex without love.

Yes, they'd had sex once already, but at the time she'd been under the delusion that he loved her and had proposed to her out of genuine emotion. Which was very different from the business arrangement he'd presented to her earlier.

His lips lowered over hers again, but she pulled back, heart thumping. "Stop, Jake. I'm not ready."

His eyes darkened. "Why not?"

"It's all happening too fast. I still barely know who I am. I can't think straight with you kissing me."

"Maybe I don't want you to think straight." A gleam shone in his seductive dark eyes.

"That's what I'm worried about." She tugged herself from his embrace, and almost to her surprise, he let her go. "I don't want to rush into this and realize a year or so from now that it was a huge mistake."

"I'll make sure you never regret it."

"I think that's quite arrogant of you." She tilted her chin. She'd never spoken to him like this before and it scared her a little. How would he react? "You seem to think you know exactly what I feel, and how I'll react."

"I know you very well after six years together." His warm gaze and proud, handsome face were dangerous— both familiar and alluring.

"But those were six years together in a professional relationship, not a marriage." For a start, he'd never barged into her room with his arms wrapped around her waist.

"I don't really see the difference." He looked down at her, slightly supercilious.

Indignation surged inside her, battling with the infuriating desire to kiss his sensual mouth. "That's the problem. It is different. As your assistant I have to follow certain rules of behavior, to always be polite and not express my opinion unless it's directly relevant to our work. To be on my best behavior and keep my emotions to myself. Maybe I'm not really the person you think I am at all." Her voice rose and she sounded a little hysterical.

Which was probably good, since he seemed to think she was some kind of well-mannered automaton who could easily approach the rest of her life as a kind of well-paid job with excellent benefits and perks.

"So the real Andi is very different from the one I know?"

She let out a long sigh. "Yes." She frowned. Who was the real Andi and what did she want? For so long she'd wanted Jake—while knowing in her heart that he would never be hers—that it was hard to think straight. "I don't know. But that's why we need to take it slow. You don't want to marry me and then find out I'm not the faithful and loyal helpmeet you imagine."

"I'd love to get to know your wild side." His eyes narrowed and a half smile tilted his mouth.

"I'm not sure I have one."

"You do." His smile widened, showing a hint of white teeth. "I've seen it."

Her face heated. "I still can't believe you slept with me under false pretenses." Her body stirred just at the memory of being stretched against him, skin to skin.

"They weren't false. We really are engaged."

She crossed her arms over her chest, and tried to ignore the tingling in her nipples. "I beg to differ. You hadn't asked the real me to marry you. You just assumed that I would. Not the same thing at all."

"But you seemed so happy about it." His expression was sweetly boyish for a moment, which tugged at a place deep inside her. "I thought you truly wanted us to be together."

I did.

She blinked, trying to make sense of it all. Jake's sturdy masculine presence wasn't helping one bit. She was painfully aware of the thickly muscled body under his elegant evening suit and how good it would feel pressed against hers.

He picked up her hand and kissed it. A knightly gesture no doubt intended to steal her heart. She shivered slightly as his lips pressed against the back of her hand, soft yet insistent.

During the nightmare of not knowing who she was, the one source of relief and happiness was Jake. He'd been the rock she could lean on and draw strength from while everything else around her was confusing and mysterious. She had been happy then, at least during the moments that the rest of the world fell away and they were alone together, lost in each other.

Could that happen again?

"I think we should spend some time together away from the palace." Getting out of their everyday work environment would be an interesting test of their relationship. They really hadn't spent leisure time together. Of course Jake didn't exactly have free time, unless you counted junkets with investors and state dinners. She didn't either, since she'd always devoted every minute to her job. She never went on the staff trips to the local nightclub or their weekend jaunts to Munich or Salzburg. As Jake's assistant she'd always felt herself too needed—or so she'd told herself—to disappear for more than an hour or two.

Jake stroked her hand, now held between both of his. She struggled to keep herself steady and not sink into his arms. "Is there someplace near here that you've always wanted to go?"

He tilted his head and his gaze grew distant. "The mountains."

"The ones you can see out the window?"

"Yes. I've always wanted to climb up and look down on the town and the palace." He shrugged. "There's never time."

"There isn't time right now, cither." She sighed. "I don't suppose you really can get away from the palace right before Independence Day." Her request for time alone seemed silly and petty now that she thought about it. He had a lot of work to do and people would be arriving from all over the world in the run-up to the celebrations.

"Then we'll have to make time." He squeezed her hand.

An odd sensation filled her chest. He was willing to drop everything on a whim to get away with her? "But who will greet the arriving guests? We'd be gone for hours." There was a large group of Ruthenian expats arriving from Chicago, including three prominent businessmen and their families who had been invited to stay at the palace.

"I'm sure the staff can manage. Livia's proving very capable."

A slight frisson of anxiety trickled through her. Why did the idea of Livia quietly taking over her job make her so uncomfortable? Surely it was ideal.

"And how would we get there?"

"My car." Amusement twinkled in his eyes. "I can still drive, you know, even though I rarely get the chance."

"No driver or attendant?"

"Not even a footman. And we'll leave our PDAs behind, too. No sense being halfway up a mountain texting people about trade tariffs."

Andi laughed. He really was prepared to drop everything just to make her happy. Selfish of her to want that, but it felt really good. And the mountains had always called to her. Right now the slopes below the snow-covered peaks were lush with grass and wildflowers. "We'd better bring a picnic."

"Of course. Let the kitchen know what you want and tell them to pack it in something we can carry easily."

Andi blinked. This would be a test for her of how she could handle the transformation from staff to employer.

Or as Jake's wife was she just a high-level member of staff? The situation was confusing.

She pulled her hand gently from his grasp. "When should we go?"

"Tomorrow morning. I've learned to seize the moment around here. If we wait any longer we'll get sucked into the Independence Day activities."

"I guess we should call it an early night." She hoped he'd take a hint and leave.

"But the morning is still so far off." A mischievous twinkle lit Jake's eyes.

"It's after midnight."

"One of my favorite times of day. Maybe we should go dance around on the lawn outside." His gaze swept over her elegant dress—and sent heat sizzling through the defenseless body underneath it. "You're dressed for it."

"I don't think so. I might lose my memory again." *Or just my heart.*

She did not want anything sensual to happen between them until she'd had a chance to wrap her mind around the whole situation and make some tough decisions. Jake's touch had a very dangerous effect on her common sense, and this was the rest of her life at stake here.

"Just a stroll in the moonlight?" He took a step toward her. Her nipples thickened under her bodice and heat curled low in her belly.

"No." She'd better get him out of here and away from her while she still could. It wasn't easy saying no to something you'd dreamed of for six long years. "We'll be doing plenty of walking tomorrow. Conserve your energy."

"What makes you think I need to?" He lifted a brow. Humor sparkled in his eyes.

Andi's insides wobbled. Was he really so attracted to her? It was hard to believe that he'd gone from not noticing her at all, to trying every trick in the book to lure her into his bed.

Then again, he was known for his ability to close a deal by any means necessary.

It was more important right now to learn whether he could respect her wishes, or not. This was a crucial test.

"Goodnight, Jake." She walked to the door and opened it. "I'll see you in the morning." Her pulse quickened, wondering if he'd protest and refuse to leave.

"Goodnight, Andi." He strolled to the doorway and brushed a soft kiss across her lips. No hands, thank goodness, though her body craved his touch. He pulled back and stepped into the hallway.

Her relief was mingled with odd regret that she wouldn't be spending the night in his strong arms.

He'd passed her test.

Then he turned to face her. "I have a bet for you."

"A bet? I'm not the gambling type."

"I didn't think you were." His mouth tilted into a wry smile. "But I bet you that tomorrow night you'll sleep in my bed—with me."

Her belly quivered under the force of his intense gaze, but she held herself steady. "What are the odds, I wonder?"

"I wouldn't advise betting against me." He crossed his arms over his powerful chest.

"Normally, neither would I." She couldn't help smiling.

His confidence was rather adorable. "But I think it's important to keep a clear head in this situation."

"I completely agree." He flashed his infuriating pearly grin.

His arrogance alone made her determined to resist. Apparently she'd be the one with a test to pass tomorrow.

Nine

Andi watched as two footmen loaded their picnic lunch—impractically packed in two large baskets—into the trunk of Jake's black BMW sedan. The cook had acted as if Andi was already mistress of the house. No questioning of her ideas or complaining that they were low on certain ingredients, as she usually did.

Livia managed to pass on a couple of comments from the staff gossip—including that everyone knew Jake had slept alone the previous night. Andi blushed. Of course everyone knew everything in the palace, especially the maids. Livia obviously wasn't intimidated by Andi's new status and she made it clear that Jake would have had company in bed if she were in Andi's shoes.

In the old days it would be expected for her to wait until the wedding night. Now it was quite the opposite. People would wonder what was wrong if she persisted in sleeping alone.

She'd dressed in those jeans Jake liked and a pale pink shirt she'd bought on a whim, then decided it wasn't professional enough. Her hair was in a ponytail—not as formal as the bun—and she'd forgone all makeup except blush and lip gloss.

Apparently she wanted him to find her attractive.

This whole situation was very confusing. She wanted him to want her—but only for the right reasons.

Jake strode down the steps, talking on his phone. He'd abandoned his usual tailored suit for a pair of dark jeans and a white shirt, sleeves rolled up over tanned arms. He smiled when he saw her, and her stomach gave a little dip.

Pulling the phone from his ear he switched it off and handed it to one of the footmen. "Kirk, please hold this hostage until I get back. I don't want any interruptions." He turned to Andi. "Did you leave yours behind, too?"

"It's on my desk. I can handle the challenge of being incommunicado all afternoon."

"What if you need to call for help?" asked Kirk.

"We're quite capable of helping ourselves." Jake held the passenger door open for Andi. She climbed in, anticipation jangling her nerves. She couldn't remember being anywhere all alone with Jake. She felt safe with him though. He'd be a match for any wolves or bears or whatever mythical creatures stalked the mountains of Ruthenia.

He climbed in and closed the door. In the close quarters of the car he seemed bigger than usual, and his enticing male scent stirred her senses. His big hand on the stick shift made her belly shimmy a little. "How do you get so tanned?"

"Tennis. We should play it sometime."

Of course. He played with any guests who showed an interest, and invariably won. He was far too naturally competitive to be diplomatic while playing a sport.

"I haven't played since college."

"I bet you were good." He shot her a glance.

"I wasn't too bad." Her nerves tingled with excitement at the prospect of playing with him. There was something they had in common. Of course he'd beat her, but she'd enjoy the challenge of taking even a single point off him. "We'll have to give it a try."

If I stay.

They pulled out of the large wrought-iron gates at the end of the palace driveway and past the old stone gatehouse. Andi waved to the guards, who nodded and smiled. Somehow living here as Jake's...partner didn't feel all that odd right now.

It felt downright possible.

"Do you know which roads to take to get to the foot of the mountain?"

"I know which roads to take to get halfway up the mountain, and that's where we're headed."

"Don't like climbing?"

"I love it, but why not climb the high part?"

Andi laughed. "That sounds like a good approach to life in general."

"I think so."

They drove through the ancient village, where some of the buildings must be a thousand years old, with their sloping tile roofs and festoons of chimneys. The road widened as they left the village and headed through a swathe of meadows filled with grazing cows. The sun was rising into the middle of an almost cloudless sky and the whole landscape looked like a 1950s Technicolor movie. She almost expected Julie Andrews to come running down a hillside and burst into song.

"What would you have done if you were born to be king of somewhere really awful?"

Jake laughed. "Everywhere has its merits."

"Antarctica."

"Too many emperors there already—the kind with flippers. But I see your point. Still, a lot of people said Ruthenia was too badly broken to be fixed. Years of decline during and after the fall of communism, no work ethic, low morale and motivation. And it's turned on its head in three short years since independence. You just have to believe."

"And work hard."

"No denying that. But when you have concrete goals and a good road map, almost anything is doable."

The sunlight pouring through the windshield played off his chiseled features. His bone structure alone contained enough determination for a small, landlocked nation.

He'd been totally up-front about his goals and road map where she was concerned. The goal was obviously a long and successful marriage that would help him as a monarch, and the road map apparently included seducing her into his bed tonight.

She was not going to let him do that. Her judgment was already clouded enough by his sturdy, masculine presence in the car next to her.

The car started to climb steadily, as the road wound around the base of the mountain. It looked much bigger from here, the snow-capped peak now invisible above a band of conifers that ringed the mountain's middle like a vast green belt. The road petered out into a steep farm track past a group of cottages, then finally ended at a field gate about a mile farther on.

"We're on our own from here." Jake climbed out and popped the trunk. "And since we don't have sherpas, we'd better eat lunch close by. These baskets look like they were designed for royal picnics in the nineteenth century."

"They probably were." Andi touched the soft leather

buckles on the big, wicker rectangles. She and Jake carried one together through the gate and into the field. Distant sheep ignored them as they spread their blanket under a tree and unpacked the feast.

Jake took the lid off the first dish. "Cabbage rolls, very traditional." He grinned. She had a feeling he'd appreciate her picking a Ruthenian dish. The spicy meat wrapped in soft boiled cabbage was as Ruthenian as you could get, and there was a jar of the hot dipping pickle and onion sauce served with it at Ruthenian inns. Jake picked up a perfectly wrapped cabbage roll and took a bite. "Ah. New Yorkers have no idea what they're missing out on. We really should market this for the States."

"Do you ever stop thinking about business?" She raised a brow.

"Truthfully? No. But then you know that already." His eyes twinkled as he took another bite.

At least he was honest. Andi reached into another dish and pulled out one of the tiny phyllo pastry wraps filled with soft, fresh goat cheese. This one came with a dish of tangy beetroot sauce. She spooned the sauce onto her pastry and took a bite. Like many things in Ruthenia it was surprising and wonderful. "These would definitely be a big hit. Perhaps a Ruthenian restaurant in Midtown."

"To give the Russian Tea Room a run for its money?" Jake nodded and took a phyllo wrap. "I like the way you think. You can't deny that we're a good team."

Her heart contracted a little. "Yes." A good team. They were that. But was that enough? She wanted more. She wanted...magic.

The midday sun sparkled on the roofs of the town far below them. "Why didn't they build the castle up here? It would have been easier to defend."

"It would also have been really hard getting a cartloads of supplies up and down that steep track."

"I guess the peasants would have had to carry everything."

"And maybe they would have staged a revolt." Jake grinned, and reached for a spicy Ruthenian meatball. "Easier to build on the flat and put a town nearby."

"As an imported peasant I have to agree."

Jake laughed. "You're the king's fiancée. That hardly makes you a peasant."

"Don't think I'll forget my humble peasant origins." She teased and sipped some of the sweet bottled cider they'd bought. "I'm the first person in my family to go to college, after all."

"Are you really? What do your parents do?"

Andi swallowed. So odd that they hadn't talked about her past or her family before now. Jake had never been interested. "My dad works at a tire dealership and my mom runs the cafeteria at a local elementary school."

Jake nodded and sipped his cider. Was he shocked? Maybe he'd assumed her dad was a lawyer and her mom a socialite. Discomfort prickled inside her. "Your ancestors would probably be scandalized that you're even thinking of marrying someone like me."

"I bet the old Ruthenian kings married the miller's daughter or a pretty shepherd girl from time to time."

"Maybe if they could spin straw into gold," Andi teased. "Otherwise they probably just had affairs with them and married girls who came with large estates and strategically located castles."

He laughed. "You're probably right. But you can spin straw into gold, can't you?"

"I find that spinning straw into freshly minted Euros is more practical these days." She bit off a crunchy mouthful of freshly baked Ruthenian pretzel, fragrant with poppy seeds. "Gold makes people suspicious."

Jake smiled. Andi really did make gold, at least in his life. "If only people knew that you're the dark secret behind the salvation of the Ruthenian economy. Sitting up there in your office at your spinning wheel."

"They probably figure I must have mysterious powers. Otherwise why wouldn't you marry a Ruthenian glamour girl?"

"Those Ruthenian ladies are all a handful. None of them grew up in Ruthenia, either. I'd like to know what they're doing in those Swiss finishing schools to produce such a bunch of spoiled, self-indulgent princesses. They're far too much like hard work, and you'd certainly never catch them doing any real work." And none of them had Andi's cute, slightly freckled nose.

She looked pleased. "They can't all be like that."

"The ones who aren't are off pursuing careers some-where—probably in the U.S.—and aren't hanging around the palace trying to curry favor with me."

"You could have staged a campaign to invite all Ruthenian expats to come back and compete for your hand."

Jake shuddered at the thought. "Why would I want to do that when you're right here?" He took a bite of a pretzel. "You've already passed every possible kind of test life in Ruthenia has thrown at you and proved yourself a star."

She blushed slightly. "I wouldn't say that."

"I would." His chest filled with pride that Andi had managed the big shift in lifestyle with such grace and ease. She'd eased the transition for him in so many ways that he'd probably never even know. No one could deny they were a powerful team. "Let's drink to us."

She took a glass with a slightly shaky hand. "To us."

"And the future of Ruthenia." Which would be a very bright one, at least for him, with the lovely Andi at his side. He'd seen another side of her since her memory came back—a feistier, more independent Andi than the one who'd worked so tirelessly as his assistant. He liked her all the more for being strong enough to stand up to him.

And the chemistry between them…if that's what it was. He couldn't put it into words, but the very air now seemed to crackle with energy when they got a little too close. He hoped she felt it, too—and suspected she did. Her cheeks colored sometimes just when he looked at her, and there was a new sparkle in her lovely blue eyes—or maybe it had always been there and he'd just never noticed it before?

Obviously he'd been walking through life with blinkers on where Andi was concerned. Thank heavens he'd finally realized what he'd been missing out on all these years.

After they'd finished eating they packed the baskets back in the car and set off up the grassy slopes on foot. The meadows grew steeper as they climbed, and the view more magnificent. They could see over the ancient forest on the far side of the town, and to the hills beyond, with villages scattered in the valleys, church steeples rising up from their midst. Jake's heart swelled at the sight of his beautiful country, so resilient and hopeful.

"Thank you for bringing us up here." He wanted to touch her, to hold her and kiss her and share the joy that pulsed through him, but Andi managed to remain out of reach.

After about an hour of steady climbing, they reached a small round tower, almost hidden in a grove of trees.

"Yikes. I wonder if the witch still has Rapunzel imprisoned in there." Andi peered up at the gray stones, mottled with moss and lichens.

"It's a lookout post," he replied. "I've seen it on the old

maps. They would watch for soldiers approaching in the distance, then signal down to the palace—which was a fortified castle back then—with a flag that let them know what was happening. Let's go inside."

He strode ahead into the arched doorway. Andi followed, rather more hesitant.

"There was probably a door, but it's gone," she said as she peered up into the tower. Any ceiling or upper floors were also gone, and the stone walls circled a perfect patch of blue sky. "It would make a great play fort for kids."

"We'll have to refurbish it for ours." Jake smiled. He'd never given much thought to having children, but the prospect of sharing family life with Andi stirred something unexpected and warm inside him.

Andi's eyes widened.

"Have I shocked you?"

"Maybe. It's all just a bit…sudden."

Jake shrugged. His changed relationship with Andi felt surprisingly natural, as if it had been in the cards the whole time without him knowing it, almost in the same way he was destined to return to Ruthenia.

But one thing still pricked at him. She'd been planning to take off—to abandon him and Ruthenia in search of… what? "Why were you going to leave?"

She startled slightly. "I already told you. I didn't see any future in my job and I felt it was time to move on."

He frowned. He couldn't help but feel there was more to it than that. "What were you going to do, back in the States?" He walked toward her. Sunlight pouring through the open roof illuminated her hair with a golden halo and cast sunbeams over her slender form.

"Um, I was thinking of starting my own business."

Shock and hurt surprised him. Her leaving still felt like

a personal betrayal. "Intriguing. What kind of business?" She could start her business here.

"Event planning. I intended to find a job at an event-planning company, then gradually branch out on my own."

"You've certainly got the experience for it."

"I know." She lifted her chin. "I must have planned hundreds of events over the last six years."

She wanted to be independent, in charge of her own destiny. He admired that. "As queen you'll have significant responsibilities. You'll be an important person in your own right. People will request your presence for events I can't attend." He knew she'd find it fulfilling.

"It's hardly the same." She lifted her chin. "I'd still be working for you."

"Working *with* me." He took a step toward her. "As equals." Another step. She hadn't moved. He reached out and took her hand. His skin hummed as their fingers met.

"You shouldn't," she breathed, tensing at his touch. "I really was planning to leave, and I still might."

His chest tightened, though he didn't really believe her. "You'll have a wonderful life here. You already know that. You'll never be bored and you can run all the businesses you want, as well as being queen." He stroked her hand with his thumb. Her skin was so soft.

"I still don't believe that staying is the right thing to do."

"I'll convince you." Pride mingled with emotion coursed through him as he raised her hand to his mouth and pressed his lips to her palm.

She gasped slightly and tried to pull her hand back, but he held it fast.

Her lips quivered slightly as his moved closer. Her delicious scent tormented his senses. He eased toward her until their chests were almost touching. She still hadn't moved. He could see in her darkening gaze that she felt the same fierce attraction he did. She wanted him every bit as much as he wanted her, despite her foolish worries and reservations. He'd just have to prove to her that her future should be right here, with him.

His lips closed over hers in a single swipe that drew them together. She arched into him, and he felt her nipples tighten inside her blouse as her fingertips clutched at his crisp shirt. She kissed him back hard, running her fingers into his hair and down his collar.

Jake sighed, reveling in the glorious sensation of holding Andi tight in his arms and kissing her doubts away.

She shuddered as his hand slid over her backside and down her thigh. Her knees buckled slightly as he touched her breast with his other hand, squeezing gently through her soft blouse.

No denying the energy between them. It had a life force of its own and drew them closer and bound them more tightly together every time they touched.

She shivered as his hand roamed under her blouse and his fingers brushed her taut nipple through her bra. At the same time his tongue flicked hers in a way that made her gasp.

Jake grimaced. He'd grown painfully hard. The sheer pleasure of kissing Andi was rather undermined by the powerful urge to strip off her clothes and make mad, passionate love to her right here, right now.

But he didn't want to drive her away. He'd already pushed too far too fast and he needed to let her come to him—to leave her wanting more.

He eased his mouth from hers and left her blinking in the half light of the tower as he pulled back. "Let's not get carried away. It's not too comfortable in here."

When he took things further, he needed to be sure she'd say yes. It was a delicate dance and he didn't entirely want her to know how much power she had over him. She could use it against him. The last nights alone had been painful and he had no intention of prolonging the torment by coming on too strong. He couldn't risk losing her now.

They walked a little higher up the mountain, then decided they'd scaled lofty enough heights for one day and turned for home. A bit out of character for him. Normally if he started something he had to take it as far as it could go.

In the car on the way back he realized he was going to forfeit his bet. Yes, he could seduce her on a whim—her reaction in the tower proved that. But he no longer wanted to. He wanted her heart and mind entwined with his, not just her body, so winning a bet seemed meaningless in the grand scheme of things.

It was a sign of maturity to forfeit a battle in order to win the war. He kissed her good-night with chaste tenderness, and watched her walk away to her own room with regret and desire singing in his blood.

Andi couldn't help a tiny twinge of guilt when she awoke in the morning and remembered that she'd made him lose his bet.

The kiss in the tower had shocked and scared her. How easily she fell into his arms, panting and moaning and letting him know just how easily her control evaporated around him. If he hadn't broken off the kiss she'd probably have made love to him right there on the moss-covered stones.

All that talk about their children and her future as queen had mingled with his powerful touch to throw her into a swoon of excitement, and at that point she might have agreed to anything just to feel his body against hers.

Not good.

She needed to think with her head, and not with her heart. Or any other parts of her body. Jake was still Jake—all business, all about Ruthenia, practical and not personal. He'd never for one instant hinted that he loved her. He was too much of a gentleman to lie about something like that.

She shivered, despite the morning sun. Why did she have to be so crazy about him?

It was the last day before the Independence Day celebrations turned Ruthenia into a countrywide party. She knew they'd both be flat-out busy today making last-minute plans and it should be easy to avoid him.

At least until tonight.

A tiny ray of pride shone through her anxiety. She'd managed to resist him after all, which meant she could still be clearheaded about her choice to stay or go. After the kiss in the tower she hadn't been so sure.

She showered and dressed, hoping she could manage not to be alone with him too much today. Her schedule—so recently abandoned—was packed with things to organize for the festivities. Plans made long before his crazy idea of marrying her, and which she couldn't really trust to anyone else.

Or that she didn't want to.

"Hey, Andi." A voice through the door made her jump. Not Jake's voice. Livia's. "Want me to take over for you so you can spend the day with His Majesty?"

"Not at all. I have everything covered." She hurried to the door and pulled it open, glad she'd painted on her usual business face. "I'll run through the guest list and make sure plans are in place to receive all the dignitaries arriving today. If you could check the menus and make any adjustments based on availability, I'd appreciate that."

A smile pulled at Livia's mouth. "You don't have to do all this stuff anymore, you know."

"This is the biggest occasion in Ruthenia's history—since independence, anyway, and I intend to pull my weight." And keep as busy and as far away from Jake as possible.

"I can handle it." Livia crossed her arms.

"I'm sure you have plenty of other things to handle." Would Livia offer to handle Jake, as well? Andi felt sure she'd be happy to take charge of his very personal needs, if requested. A twinge of jealousy tweaked her. "I have some phone calls to make."

She spent the day running from her office to the various meeting rooms and dining rooms, making last-minute changes to travel schedules and setting up tours of the local area for the visitors. Around lunchtime, visitors started to trickle in, arriving in their diplomatic cars and in hired limos, and she welcomed them to the palace.

Of course she welcomed them as Jake's fiancée, and the congratulations rang painfully in her ears as guest after guest remarked on how happy they were for the royal couple.

Jake looked rather pleased and proud, but then maybe he always looked like that. Twice he managed to slide his arm around her in situations where it would have been embarrassing to resist. Once in front of the French ambassador, and another time while greeting the Taiwanese cultural attaché. She cursed the way her skin hummed and sizzled under his touch, even through her tailored suit.

The big ring glittered on her finger, like a sign saying, Property of the Palace.

But Jake didn't own her. She hadn't agreed to marry him, simply to stay until after the celebrations.

At least that's what she tried to tell herself.

Feelings of foreboding and guilt, that she'd let down the

entire country as well as Jake, gathered in her chest like a storm. Could she really leave?

If it meant escaping a lifetime of heartache, yes.

Ten

This was it, his last chance. Jake eyed Andi from the far end of the long table, over the sparkling crystal and polished plates of the state dinner. Tomorrow was Independence Day and he could feel in his gut that he still hadn't convinced her to stay.

Why was she so stubborn?

She knew how many women would give a limb to be in her position, but she didn't seem to value the role of queen at all. Andi wasn't interested in wearing inherited diamonds or dressing up in silk and lace. She didn't care about dining with international luminaries or being called Your Majesty. She cared about people, regardless of whether they were important or not.

All of which only made him like her more.

And then there was that face. Curious and intelligent, with that active mouth and slightly upturned nose. Those sharp blue eyes that never missed anything.

And her slim but strong body, which beckoned him from beneath her fitted golden dress. Tonight he would claim her and sleep with her in his arms, assured that she'd never leave him.

He danced with her three times—heat crackling through his veins—while the jazz quartet played in the ballroom. In between, while dancing with other women, he barely took his eyes off her.

"I'm afraid Andi and I must retire," he announced, after the shortest decent amount of time. He didn't want to give her a chance to escape. "We've got a big day tomorrow, so I'm sure you'll excuse us."

He strode toward her and took her arm, then swept her out of the ballroom. She stiffened once they exited the soft lighting and sensual music, and entered the gilt-trimmed hallway.

"I'm exhausted," she murmured, avoiding his gaze.

"No, you're not." Not yet. He slid his hand along her back and saw the way her nipples peaked under the fine silk of her gown. A flush spread from her cheeks to her neck.

Desire flashed through him at this fresh confirmation that she wanted him as badly as he wanted her.

And he was going to make sure neither of them was disappointed.

"You're coming with me." He tightened his arm around her waist and marched her along the hallway.

"You can't make me." She whispered while her flushed cheeks and dark, dilated pupils argued with her words.

"I'm not going to make you do anything." Her hand felt hot in his, and desire whipped around them, distinct and intoxicating. It had been building all day. All week. For the past six years—though he'd been too wrapped up in business to notice it until now.

He opened the door to his suite and tugged her inside.

Then closed and locked it. Her mouth opened in protest, lips red, and he kissed her words away.

She struggled slightly—a token resistance he'd expected—before she softened and her arms closed around him as he knew they would. Once again he felt her fingertips press into the muscle of his back—claiming him—and he grew hard as steel against her.

Andi's soft body felt like a balm to his aching soul. Her mouth tasted like honey and sunshine, and her skin was warm and soothing. His fingers roamed into the silk of her hair and down over her gentle curves.

She writhed, and a gentle sigh slid from her lips as he cupped her breast. He could feel the connection between them, invisible and powerful, and he knew she could feel it, too, when she let down her resistance.

Her dress came off easily, via a simple zipper concealed behind a row of false buttons. Pleasure rippled through his muscles as the luxurious fabric pulled away, revealing soft lace and even softer skin.

Groaning, he settled her onto the bed and pressed a line of kisses over her chin and neck, then down between her breasts and over her belly, which twitched as he roamed lower, burying his face in the lace of her panties.

He felt her fingertips in his hair and heard her low moan as he sucked her through the delicate fabric and enjoyed the heat of her arousal. Her legs wrapped around his shoulders, pulling him closer into her and he licked her to a state of silky wetness before slipping the delicate lingerie down over her smooth thighs.

"You're so beautiful." He murmured the words as his eyes feasted on her lush nakedness. All wide, blue-eyed innocence, her gaze met his for a second before she reached for him and pulled him over her, kissing him with ferocity that snatched his breath and tightened his muscles.

Struggling together they removed his formal suit, baring his hot skin. Aroused almost to the point of insanity after these past days of torture, he couldn't wait to be inside her.

And the feeling was mutual. Andi raised her hips, welcoming him as she breathed hot kisses over his face and neck. Sinking into her again was the best feeling he'd ever had. He guided them into a shared rhythm that made Andi gasp and moan with pleasure.

He wanted Andi at his side—and in his bed—for the rest of his life. She was perfect for him in every way. Brilliant, beautiful, sensual and loyal.

He eased them into another position that deepened the connection between them and made beads of delicious perspiration break out on Andi's brow. Her breathing was ragged and her lips formed an ecstatic smile. Pleasure swelled in both of them, thickening and deepening and growing into something new—their future together—as they moved together, clinging to each other with fevered desperation.

Jake held his climax off for as long as he could, until Andi's cries reached a pitch of pleasured anguish that sent him over the edge. They collapsed onto the bed together, panting and laughing, then relaxed into a sleepy embrace.

A sense of deep contentment settled over him, along with the languid desire unfurled in his limbs. Emotions he couldn't name flickered through him and illuminated his visions of the happy future they'd share, as he drifted off to a peaceful sleep.

Andi watched Jake's chest rise and fall, while silver beams of moonlight caressed his skin through a crack in the curtains. Her heart swelled with painful sensation.

It had been so easy. She'd told him she was tired and that

she wanted to go to bed. Did he care? No. He had his own agenda and her needs were irrelevant.

He also knew she never had a prayer of resisting him. How could one person have so much power over her? He'd ruled her life for six years. Six years during which the joy of being with Jake was mingled readily with the sorrow of knowing their relationship was strictly business.

Now he'd followed through on his promise to seduce her into his bed. He'd driven her half mad with sensation—just because he could—and now he slept like a newborn, without an ounce of recrimination.

If only life could be that simple for her.

He didn't care if she loved him or not. That didn't matter to him one bit. He needed a wife and she was a promising candidate with a good résumé. Tried and tested, even, in more ways than one.

Jake probably didn't want to love anyone. Emotions were complicated and messy, and he wouldn't like anyone else having that kind of power over him. No doubt he preferred to keep things clearheaded and businesslike.

At least for one more day, she could manage to do the same. She couldn't bear to think ahead any further than that right now.

The next morning, Andi helped Jake host a palace breakfast for nearly fifty guests. Then they rode through the town in an open carriage with a procession of schoolchildren in front and the town's marching band behind them. Flags waved from windows and hands and the whole country seemed alive with enthusiasm and energy.

At one point Jake slid his hand into hers and warmth flared in Andi's chest at the affectionate gesture. But she turned to look at him and he was waving out the window with the other hand. No doubt the romantic gesture was just intended to look picturesque to the gathered crowds.

Her heart ached that she wanted so much more than a relationship put on for show.

Back at the palace a feast filled long tables on the patio outside the ballroom. She had her work cut out for her chatting with female guests—each of whom congratulated her on her engagement and wished her every happiness.

Are you happy? she wanted to ask each of them. Did these elegant women in their designer clothes enjoy close and loving relationships with their important husbands? Or were they content to follow along and smile, enjoying the gourmet food and expensive shoes that came with the job?

She envied the few women who were there in their own right as ambassadors or dignitaries of sorts. In charge of their own destinys and not dependent on anyone.

Whenever she glimpsed Jake, he looked right at home amidst the glamorous crowd, smiling and talking and laughing—in his element.

By midafternoon Andi felt exhausted. Last night's late-night shenanigans hadn't helped. As servants cleared the coffee cups and the guests wandered out onto the lawn, she slipped back into the palace for a moment's breather.

"Hey, Your Majesty." Livia's voice startled her as she hurried along the corridor. "Playing hooky?"

"Getting something from my room." She just wanted to be alone.

"Don't you have servants for that?" Livia's brown eyes twinkled with mischief as she caught up with Andi and followed close by her.

"I'm used to doing things for myself."

"It must be hard to make the leap from PA to princess. Though I think I could manage it." She crossed her arms.

"Shame Jake didn't notice me first. Still, maybe it's not too late." She raised a brow. "I don't imagine kings usually stick to one woman for the rest of their lives."

"Have you lost your mind?" Andi's temper finally snapped. She ran up the stairs, hoping Livia would not follow.

Livia laughed, climbing right behind her. "Oh, dear. We have turned into a princess, haven't we? I'm just saying what I've observed. It must be difficult watching your fiancé dance with other women almost every night. It takes a special person to put up with that, I'd imagine."

"It's just part of his job."

"And I suppose that putting up with it is part of yours." Livia followed her down the hallway to her own door. "Oh, dear, will I get fired for speaking my mind?"

Her voice grated on Andi's nerves. "Quite possibly."

"You must feel pretty powerful right now."

Not in the least. She wanted to cry. If she was just Jake's assistant she'd have had no difficulty issuing Livia some task, then talking later to Jake about how she wasn't working out. Now, somehow, everything seemed more loaded.

More personal.

"Don't you have a job to do?" Andi turned to her. "There's a big event going on and you should be running it."

"You should be attending it, so I guess we're both skiving off. I'm leaving anyway. Off to New York." She grinned and crossed her arms.

Curiosity goaded Andi. "You have a job there?"

"You'd know all about it. It's the one I told you about that you tried to steal from me. I guess it's lucky for both of us that I tripped you on those stairs in your silly dress."

"What?" Shock washed over her. "Is that when I hit my head?"

"Oh, did I just say that out loud?" She shook her head, making her red curls dance. "Must be loopy from packing. Certainly was lucky, though! I'd have said 'have a nice trip' if I'd known I was sending you into King Jake's affectionate arms. I saw you dancing around like a loon and him coming to your rescue."

Andi stared at her. "I think you should leave right this minute before I tell someone you tried to hurt me."

Livia just laughed. "I couldn't agree more. I'm looking forward to leaving this sleepy backwater and getting back to the big city. Ah, freedom!"

Anger flashed through Andi as Livia waltzed away. None of this would have happened if it wasn't for her interfering jealousy!

She couldn't help being jealous of Livia, now. If Andi married Jake she'd never get to live in New York again. Never be mistress of her own destiny again, with plans and hopes and dreams that could change on a whim.

She'd have duties. Responsibilities. She'd have to be loyal and faithful, serving Ruthenia and Jake until the end of her days.

While Jake danced and flirted and chatted with other women, day after day, night after night.

At least Livia wouldn't be around to taunt her anymore.

In the bathroom she splashed water on her face. She looked pale and haunted, so she slapped on a bit of her familiar blush. But even that couldn't pick up her spirits right now, though. She'd been in the public eye all day, and even though Jake was right there at her side for much of the time, it felt as if they were a thousand miles apart—her craving affection and love, and him needing a royal spouse to put on for ceremonial occasions, much like his sash and scepter.

Last night's intimacy didn't make things better. The closeness they'd shared for those brief hours seemed so distant now, like it wasn't real at all. The memory of his embrace still made her heart beat faster, which only made it hurt more that he didn't love her.

Were her suitcases still here under the bed? Sudden curiosity prompted her to look. They were. She'd only committed to stay through the end of today. After that she could pack her things—again—and get back on the track she'd planned before Jake derailed her for his own professional needs.

A wife by Independence Day. That's all he'd needed. If she wasn't around, he might well have asked Livia. It probably didn't matter all that much to him as long as she did her job.

Still, she did have a job to do for today. She dabbed on a little of her favorite scent, hoping it would lift her spirits. Didn't work.

Lying in his arms last night had been so bittersweet. A dream come true, but with the knowledge that it was just a dream. He'd slept with her to win her over to his side, much as he'd done while her memory was gone.

Any pleasure she'd enjoyed withered away when she remembered that.

She dabbed a bit of powder on her nose—it suddenly looked red—and steeled herself to go back downstairs again. She'd pushed herself through enough long and tiring events over the past six years; she could manage one more, even if her heart was breaking.

"Where's your fiancée?" Maxi sidled up to Jake as a waiter refilled his champagne glass.

"Andi's around somewhere. It's a big crowd." Where was she? He'd been so wrapped up in their guests he'd only glimpsed her a couple of times through the crowd. Still, they'd spent a full hour together this morning being dragged through the town in the ceremonial carriage. Andi had been quiet, which was fine with him. He liked that she didn't have to chatter on all the time like some women. He hadn't stopped thinking about her all day, wanting to see her smile, her frown, hear her laugh and even her scolding. She was becoming an obsession.

"Daddy has a proposition for you."

"Oh?" Jake sipped his freshly filled glass.

Maxi nattered on about some proposed factory project in the eastern hills. He was used to listening with one side of his brain and making the right noises, while using the other side of his brain to plan ahead.

Tonight he needed to let Andi know how much she meant to him. He'd told her with his body, but Andi was a pragmatist and he knew she'd want to hear it in words.

I love you.

The truth rang through him like the old church bell tolling in the distance. Maybe he'd known it all along but not realized it until right now. The reality of it left him stunned and filled with a powerful sense of joy.

He loved her and he had to let her know that.

"What?"

He didn't realize he'd said the words aloud until he looked into Maxi's startled face. Her lipstick-painted mouth stretched into a wide smirk. "Thank you, Jake, I'm touched."

He schooled his face into a neutral expression. "Don't take it personally." He raised a brow. "I'm talking about the development project." He must be losing it. Andi had cracked open some tender new part of him that didn't quite know how to act. He was so used to being all business all the time that it was hard to switch off that part of him and just be.

Andi certainly didn't have trouble reining her emotions in. She acted as if she was trying to decide whether to accept a promotion or not. It stung that she had no personal feelings for him at all. He could be alarmed that one slender woman had such a strong hold over him—instead he just wanted to kiss her again.

Andi stood there for a moment, incredulous. A cold, empty space opened up inside her. If Jake loved Maxi, why didn't he just marry her?

She stepped backward, shrinking back into the crowd before Maxi noticed her. Jake couldn't love Maxi, could he? She was insufferably arrogant and annoying—he'd said so himself. Unless he was just trying to throw her off the scent.

Maybe he didn't really love Maxi but just said that to her to keep her favor now that he intended to marry someone else. Maybe he was going around telling every girl in Ruthenia that he loved them and if only he didn't need a wife who can type and file efficiently...

Her mind boggled.

Jake was a master manipulator; that was how he accomplished so much and managed to get so many people on his side. Now he was masterminding his marriage, and his relationships with every beauty in the nation, with the easy grace she'd always admired.

Except that now she was its victim. So easy to seduce. Such a quiet and willing accomplice. Ready to sacrifice her life in his service.

Except that she had no intention of making that sacrifice.

She'd tell him why she was leaving, and give him a chance to reply, but nothing he said could now change her decision to get away before she signed up for a lifetime of heartache.

She made it through the grand afternoon tea and an enormous dinner. She barely saw Jake at all, so the hardest part was accepting the continued stream of congratulations on her engagement. She wanted to tell them, "I'm not marrying him!" but she didn't. Too well trained in royal decorum for that.

No. She waited until the last guests had left or gone to bed and she was alone with Jake. She let him lead her to his suite, steeling herself against the false reassurance of his hand around hers or his warm smiles.

Once inside she closed the door. "Independence Day is over, and I'm leaving."

Jake's expression turned dark. "You can't be serious."

"I am, and I'll tell you why." She straightened her shoulders and dared herself to look him right in the eye. He might have power over her, but she was stronger. "You don't love me."

"I do. I love you. I've been meaning to tell you." His expression was the same as always, bright and good-humored. Like none of this really mattered.

"But you forgot?" She forced a laugh, though inside she was crumbling to pieces. "You have been busy, of course. I overheard you telling Maxi you loved her. Perhaps you got us confused for a moment."

Jake smiled. "That's exactly what happened. I said it to you in my mind and it came out of my mouth in front of Maxi."

"You must really think I'm a total idiot." Anger snapped through her at his ludicrous response. "I know I've been pretty gullible, believing that we're engaged when we're not, and going along with your oh-so-convenient plan to get engaged in time for the big day, but it's all stopping right here."

"Andi, be sensible. It's been a long day."

"I'm tired of being sensible. I've been sensible to the point of madness lately, smiling at strangers while they congratulate me on an engagement I fully intend to break off. It's enough to drive almost anyone stark mad."

"I do love you." Jake's dark eyes fixed on hers and the intense look in them almost made her weaken.

Almost, but not quite.

"No you don't!" Her voice rose. "I don't think you even know what love is. All your relationships are carefully orchestrated for maximum effect. You stage manage us just like the seating plans at your dinners, swapping and changing people to curry favor when needed."

"I'm not trying to curry favor with you."

"Obviously not. I was seated as far as possible from you all day." She enjoyed the retort. "Maybe royal couples are supposed to be kept apart so they don't get tired of each other."

"You know that's just convention. You and I already have a close, intimate relationship."

"No, we don't." She cursed the way his words made her chest swell. "Just because you've seduced me into bed does not mean we're intimate. You think you can fix everything with sex. If you pleasure me in bed then somehow it will turn into a love that isn't there. It doesn't work like that. True intimacy is based on trust, and I don't trust you."

He stared at her, the good humor draining from his face. "I know I broke your trust. I promise you I'll never do anything to lose it again."

"Once lost, trust cannot be regained. Whether you love Maxi or not, I really don't care, but either way, I can't trust you and I won't live my life with someone when I don't know if I can believe what they say. It's too late."

Just the fact that she could even suspect him of carrying on with another woman made marriage to him a recipe for disaster.

"I want a normal life that isn't under any spotlights. I'd like to marry an ordinary man who doesn't have glamorous women kissing up to him all day." Did she? She couldn't imagine being involved with anyone after having her heart pummeled by this whole experience. She needed to get out of here before she burst into embarrassing tears.

"I've told you I love you." His features hardened and his eyes narrowed. Silence hung in the room for an agonizing moment. "I've given you ample proof that I care about you and think you're the perfect wife, yet you persist in wanting to leave. Leave then." His gaze pierced right through her. "I won't hold you here."

Andi swallowed. Now he was dismissing her.

Isn't that what she wanted? She'd already told him there was no chance. "I can't be the perfect wife for a man who really just wants a permanent assistant."

"Naturally." He seemed to look down on her along the length of his aristocratic nose. His eyes flashed dark fire. "I don't want you to marry me against your will."

"Good, because I don't think that would be right for either of us." Was she trying to convince him, or herself? "It's important to marry someone you care about. Someone you love." Her voice cracked on the word love.

Once she'd have thought she had enough love in her for Jake to sustain both of them, but lately she'd learned different. She couldn't stand by as the faithful wife while he continued to flirt with and cajole other women, even if it was just for "business" reasons. Not if she didn't know that alone, in bed, he was all hers, heart and soul.

She needed a man she'd believe when he said, "I love you."

"Goodbye, Jake." Her whispered words hovered in the night air of his dimly lit room. She pulled the big engagement ring from her finger and left it on the table.

He didn't respond. Obviously she was worth nothing to him now that she'd scuppered his neat plans. No more protestations of love, or even of how useful their union would be to Ruthenia.

Nothing but his icy glare.

Andi let herself out of the room and hurried along the corridor, grim sensations of regret trickling over her like cold water. She half hoped—and feared—that she'd hear the door open and sense Jake's powerful stride covering the carpet after her.

But nothing disturbed the small, nighttime noises of the palace.

She had to leave right now, even though there were no trains until morning. She didn't want to see him ever again.

Tears streamed down her face as she shoved her clothes back into her two suitcases for the second time in a week. How had she let herself get sucked into such an insane situation? Something about Jake Mondragon undermined all her good sense and left her gasping and starry-eyed. She'd already spent years hoping he'd suddenly fall madly in love with her, which was no doubt why his ridiculous and unsuitable engagement idea had been so easy to put over on her.

Her face heated at the thought of how happy she'd been back when she had no idea that their whole engagement wasn't genuine. He'd smiled at her and kissed her and held her like they were madly in love, knowing all along that the whole thing was a lie.

How humiliating.

She threw her hairbrush into her suitcase with a pleasant thud. Almost done with the packing. Her clothes would be really crumpled now after being shoved in so haphazardly, but she could iron them out again.

Shame she couldn't do that with her heart. She suspected it would be crushed and creased for a long time. Possibly forever.

There was still one thing hanging in the closet. The long, floaty pale dress she'd been wearing the night she lost her memory. She let out a long breath as she remembered why she had it on. She'd brought it with her to Ruthenia thinking she'd need something smart and beautiful to wear at parties now that her boss was a king. She'd chosen it after much giggling deliberation with a girlfriend, because it made her feel like Cinderella at the ball.

She'd never worn it before that night. Since she was staff, she didn't actually attend the parties. A crisp black suit had proved to be the most suitable evening attire as she hovered around the edges of the festivities, making sure everything was running smoothly and attending to Jake's every need. Her Cinderella fantasies had remained locked in the closet, just like the dress.

She'd taken it out that one night, just to see what it would feel like to wear it. The whole palace was wrapped up in the party happening in the dining room and ballroom, so no one noticed when she walked down the stairs, tiptoeing carefully in the silver sandals she'd bought to match the dress and never worn before.

She'd walked to one of the narrow casement windows and looked out. Pale moonlight glanced off the mountains in the distance and bathed the green valley in its soft glow. She'd grown to love the rugged countryside and its fiercely independent and engaging people. The palace and its nearby town were her home now, after three years. Leaving felt like stepping out of her own life and into a big, scary unknown.

Inspired by her pretty dress, she'd wanted to take one last walk around the grounds in the moonlight, just to let her imagination run free and think about what might have been before she left for the last time. The weather was surprisingly warm for so early in the spring and the soft grass, silver with dew, begged her to walk across it.

She'd crossed the wide terrace and taken off her sandals, not wanting to get the soft leather wet or have the heels sink into the lawn. Had Livia really tripped her? That's when her memory stopped. Sometimes the steps were slippery, the stone worn smooth by the passage of feet over two hundred or more years since they were built. She could see them from her window right now.

But she would never walk down them again. No detours this time. She had to get out of here and away from Jake.

She'd since worn far more fabulous and expensive dresses, tailored right on her body by Ruthenia's finest seamstresses, and she knew that they felt like the world's stiffest armor as she moved through her ceremonial duties next to a man who didn't love her.

She turned and scanned the room to see if she'd missed anything.

Her belongings had fit so neatly into her two bags, almost as if they'd just been waiting to pack up and go. Her heart sank at the sight of her empty dressing table, the gaping closet with its almost vacant hangers. Soon someone else would live in the room, and she'd never see it again.

Now all she had to do was get out of here without being seen. She couldn't bear to explain the situation to anyone. They'd be so shocked and disappointed. Disgusted even, at how she wouldn't slot into Jake's plans for the good of the nation.

Guilt snaked through her heart, or maybe it was just grief at what she was leaving behind. The memory of Jake's face—hard and angry—would stay with her forever. She shivered and turned to pick up her bags.

Even though it was well after midnight, she'd need to sneak down the back stairs. The cleaners sometimes worked late into the night, especially after a major event. If she could make her way to the rear entrance without being seen, she could cut across the gardens to the old barnyard and take one of the runabout cars kept near the old stables for staff to share on errands.

She grabbed the handle of each bag and set off, pulse pounding. No looking back this time. The pretty dress could stay right there in the closet, along with all her romantic fantasies. They'd caused her nothing but pain.

From magical fairy-tale engagement to shocking scandal overnight. She'd have to keep her head down for, oh, the rest of her life.

She let herself into the old staircase, dimly lit by aging sconces, and hurried down the steep, winding steps, bags thumping unsteadily behind her like chasing ogres no matter how high she tried to life them.

She held her breath as she opened the heavy wood door at the bottom. It led out into the back kitchen, which was rarely used, only if they were catering a truly enormous feast—like the one today. Freshly scrubbed pots and baking trays covered the sideboard and big bowls of fruit stood on the scrubbed table ready to be sliced for breakfast, but the lights were low and she couldn't see anyone about.

Lowering her bags onto their wheels, she crept across the flagstone floor.

One the far side of the old kitchen, she could see the

door that led directly out into the kitchen garden. Before she took a step into the room, a burst of laughter made her jump. She froze, heart pounding, peering into the shadows. Voices reached her from the next room, the passage to the modern kitchen. She didn't recognize them, but the palace often hired extra caterers for big events. Were they already up, making breakfast?

She shrank back into the stairwell, but after an anxious minute, no one had appeared, so they obviously hadn't heard her. Bags lifted by her straining biceps, she crept across the floor. She lowered her bags for a moment and tried the handle—old, but well-oiled, the door slid quietly open, and cool night air rushed in.

She drew in a breath, then stepped out and closed the door quietly behind her. The click of the latch struck an ominous chord in her chest. She'd left the palace forever. She should feel happy that she'd escaped the building without being seen. Instead, she felt like a thief, leaving with stolen goods.

Which was ridiculous. She'd given years of her life to this place. Was that why it hurt so much to leave? And she wasn't gone yet. She still had to get across the grounds and past the sentries at the gatehouse.

She scanned the walled garden—a gloomy well of shadows in the cloudy moonlight—then hefted her bags past the menacing dark rectangles of the large herb beds. An arched doorway on the far side led to the stable yard, where the staff cars were parked. The ancient door creaked on its hinges as she pulled it open, and she shot a glance behind her. A lightbulb flicked on in one of the upper windows, and she held her breath for a moment. Was it Jake's window? Would he come look for her?

She cursed herself when she realized that it was on the upper, staff-only floor. Why would Jake come looking for her? He'd told her to get lost. Which was exactly what she'd wanted.

Wasn't it?

Heaviness lodged in her chest as she crept across the paved stable yard. She retrieved a key from the combination-locked box in the wall—they'd be sure to change the code tomorrow—climbed into the nearest car and started the engine.

Andi glanced up at the house to see if anyone would look outside, but no one did. Cars did come and go at all hours when the house was full of guests and there were meals to prepare. She didn't turn the lights on right away.

A sharp pang of regret shot through her as she pulled onto the wide gravel drive for the last time. A ribbon of silver in the moonlight, it led through an allée of tall trees. It was hard to believe she'd never see this beautiful place again. She certainly wouldn't be welcome back for return visits.

And she'd never see Jake again. She should be happy about that, considering what he'd done, but all the years they'd spent working side by side—and that she'd spent mooning over him and hoping for more—weighed on her mind. He was a good man at heart and she didn't wish him ill.

Don't think about him.

There was still one more gauntlet to run—the gatehouse. The guards didn't usually pay too much attention to cars leaving the palace, especially familiar staff cars, so she hoped they'd simply wave her through. She cringed, though, when she saw a uniformed figure emerge from the stone gatehouse and approach.

She cleared her throat and rolled down the window. "Hi, Eli, it's only me. Picking up a friend." The lie was the first thing that sprang to mind.

Eli simply smiled and gave her a little salute. She raised her window and drove out the palace gates for the last time, blinking back tears. In the morning, Eli and everyone else would know she'd run off into the night.

The town was deserted as she drove through it. She parked on a quiet street so she could walk the last stretch to the station. No need to advertise where she'd gone, since it would probably be hours until the first train of the morning. The staff cars were all identical Mercedes wagons and easily recognizable, and she didn't want to be too easy to find.

Not that anyone would come looking for her. She left the keys in the glove compartment. Petty crime was almost nonexistent in the town as everyone knew each other too well.

She groped in her bag for dark sunglasses. No need for strangers to see her red and puffy eyes. She wrapped a blue scarf around her head and neck. It wasn't cold but she didn't want anyone to recognize her if she could help it.

All she had to do was wait for the early-morning train to Munich, then book a flight to New York.

Her original plan had been to head to Manhattan and stay at the 92nd Street Y and temp until she could find an apartment and a job. She'd even had that promising interview set up. So, there'd been a hitch in her plans, involving all her lifelong dreams coming true and then turning into a nightmare, but she'd just have to get back on track and start rebuilding her life.

She glanced up and down the dark empty street before hurrying past the old stone buildings toward the ornate nineteenth-century train station at the edge of town.

She'd intended to leave Jake behind, and now she was doing it.

So why did it still hurt so much?

Eleven

Jake paced back and forth in his bedroom, anger and pain firing his muscles into action. His wounded pride sparked fury inside him. He'd been mad enough to lose his heart to a woman, and now she flung it back in his face.

No one had ever treated him so coldly. He'd offered her his life and she'd turned him down. He should despise her for being so heartless and cruel.

So why did the thought of facing even one day without her make his whole body ache?

He'd have to announce to the whole country—to the world—that their engagement was over. People would wonder why she left and gossip would echo around the villages for months.

But he didn't care about any of that. It was the prospect of nights without Andi's soft body in his bed. Of days lacking her bright smile. Long evenings without her thoughtful conversation.

He couldn't force her to marry him against her will. Lord knows he'd come close enough by thrusting this whole engagement on her when she was indisposed by her lack of memory.

Shame trickled over him that he'd taken advantage of her so readily. She'd been so willing—in her lack of knowledge about their true past—and it had been so wonderful. A natural extension of their happy working relationship.

Idiot. Having sex with your assistant had nothing to do with work. Why had he tried to convince himself it was okay? If he really wanted to marry her he should have waited until she got her memory back, courted her like a gentleman—or at least a conventional boyfriend—then proposed to her.

Maybe he thought that as a king he was so special he didn't have to follow any of the conventions of romantic love? He certainly put a lot of energy into following other conventions, so why had he veered so badly off course with Andi?

He halted his pacing at the window. He'd been keeping an eye out for lights from a car traveling up the driveway, but had seen none. She was probably still here in the palace.

But she'd already rejected him and it was too late to change her mind. She needed a man she could trust, and in taking advantage of her amnesia, he'd given her good reason to never trust him again.

He'd given up a lot to take on his role as king of Ruthenia. Now he'd just have to learn how to live without Andi, as well.

Andi flinched as the ticket agent looked at her. She'd removed her dark glasses because, well, it was still dark outside. But there was no flicker of recognition in his eyes.

Without extravagant jewels and fancy dresses she just slipped right back into the regular population.

As the platform filled with people waiting for the first train, she shrank inside her raincoat, raising the collar. The occasional stare made her want to hide behind a column. Soon enough they'd all know who she was and what she was doing.

She climbed onto the train without incident. Had she thought Jake would send the cavalry after her? The Ruthenian hills were notably free of galloping horsemen and the roads almost empty of cars as the train pulled away from the town at 7:43 a.m.

Perhaps he was secretly relieved to see her go. He could blame her for breaking off the engagement and carry on with his merry life as an eligible royal bachelor, with gorgeous women kissing up to him at every opportunity.

Her heart still ached with jealousy at the thought of Jake with another woman. Which was totally ridiculous since she'd just rejected him.

The train picked up speed outside the town and flew through the open fields and villages with their tall steeples, clustered at the foot of the proud mountains. She'd never even heard of Ruthenia until she met Jake, but it had come to feel like home and she was going to miss it.

She pulled a book from her bag, but the words blurred before her eyes and she couldn't concentrate. Tears threatened and she pushed them back. Was she making a terrible mistake? Would Jake have grown to love her?

She'd never know now, but it was too late to turn back.

It was midmorning by the time she reached the border crossing between Ruthenia and Austria. She held her breath while the border guards walked through the train checking passports.

The young, clear-faced guard looked at her passport, then pulled out his phone. He spoke rapidly in German and made a sign to another guard on the platform. The two elderly ladies seated on the bench opposite her glanced at each other. Andi felt her heart rate rise.

"I don't have anything to declare." She gestured to her two suitcases. "You can look through them.

"Will we be moving soon?" Her voice sounded shaky. Sitting here made her feel anxious, like she wanted to get up and run. Was Jake behind this? She cursed the pinch of hope that jangled her nerves.

Unlikely. She'd never seen him look so furious as he did last night. If only she could make that memory go away.

Jake's car swerved on a gravel patch in the road and he righted it quickly, coming around another of those hairpin turns on the mountainside. He probably should have taken the train, like Andi. It was the most direct route as it cut right through one of the larger mountains.

But he didn't want anything to hold him up. He also didn't want other people around. This was between him and Andi.

His pride still hurt at her forthright rejection, but something inside him couldn't let her leave like this. She'd said she didn't trust him, and that hurt more than anything. He'd broken her trust. He'd tried to keep her at his side using seduction and bargaining.

When he told her he loved her, she simply didn't believe him.

She thought his declaration was just more words. She didn't understand that his feelings for her had transformed him.

Swinging around another tight corner, he felt a twinge of guilt about using the border guards to hold the train.

Another aspect of royal privilege he'd abused. Still, it was an emergency situation. Once she got back to the U.S., she'd be gone from his world, and he knew in his heart that he'd never get her back.

Then he'd spend the rest of his life missing her and kicking himself for losing the only woman he wanted.

He drove through the Dark Forest at warp speed, adrenaline crackling through his muscles, and emerged into the open plain on the other side just before noon. He'd had to stop on the way for one simple, but important, errand. This time he intended to get everything right.

He spotted the long train at the border crossing from quite a distance away. Luckily the road ran almost directly across the tracks near the village, so he pulled onto the verge and jumped out. Bright morning sun shone off the dark blue-and-gold surface of the cars and turned each window into a mirror. Which car was Andi in? And would she even talk to him after how he'd behaved at their last meeting? Every cell in his body, every nerve pulsed with the desperate need to see her and make things right.

The train was an old one, with individual compartments seating about six people each. The first three he peered into contained no familiar face, but in the fourth, opposite two older women in wool berets, sat a pale-faced and anxious-looking Andi.

He grasped the cool handle and inhaled. She looked up as he pushed the door open and he heard her gasp.

"I can't live without you, Andi."

He hadn't planned what to say. He'd done too much planning lately. "I really do love you." He prayed that the truth would ring through in words that now sounded hollow from overuse. "I didn't realize it myself. I've never known love before. I was raised to think with my head and not my heart. I spent so much time convincing myself I wanted to marry you because it was a sensible decision, because our marriage would be good for Ruthenia. The truth is that now my desire to keep you has nothing to do with Ruthenia. I want you for myself and I can't imagine spending the rest of my life without you."

Tears welled in her eyes for a moment and his heart clutched.

The two women opposite her suddenly rose, grabbing their carryalls, and hurried toward the door where he stood. "Please excuse us," one puttered in Ruthenian. He'd forgotten they were there. He stood aside to let them pass, eyes fixed on Andi.

She hadn't moved an inch, but color rose to her pale cheeks.

Hope flared in his chest. "I admit that our engagement began for the wrong reasons. I'm ashamed about that." Guilt stung him. "All I knew was that I enjoyed your company, and that once I kissed you…" He blew out a breath. "Once I kissed you, nothing was ever the same again."

He saw her swallow, fighting back tears that made her blue eyes glisten.

He ached to take her in his arms and kiss away her tears. The few inches between them seemed an agonizing gulf. "I need you, Andi."

Her lips didn't flinch. Her silence hurt him, but she hadn't told him to go. There was still hope.

He reached into his pocket and drew out the item he'd picked up on the way here. The simple ring, the one she'd chosen in the shop that morning.

He knelt on the floor of the train car and pulled the ring from the box. "Andi, I know this is the ring you wanted. I made you get the other one because it was showier. I realize I was making decisions for you and trying to turn you into someone you don't want to be. I'd like to go right back to the beginning and start over."

She hesitated for a moment, eyes fixed on the ring.

His heart clenched. She'd already told him that she didn't want to be his wife. She didn't want a life of royal duty and an existence in the public eye. But that wasn't all he offered. How could he make her see that despite all the trappings of royalty, he was just a man? A man who loved and needed her with every fiber of his being.

"Andi, right now I wish I wasn't a king." It took effort to stop his hands from reaching out to her. "That I could promise you an ordinary life, in a comfortable house in some American suburb, where our children could attend the local school and play in Little League. The truth is I can't. I'm already married to Ruthenia and that's my destiny. I can't turn away from it any more than I could turn back the river flowing through the mountains."

He saw her throat move as she swallowed. Her hands shifted slightly, clutching at each other through her black gloves. How he longed to take them in his own hands.

"But I need you, too, Andi. Not because you can help me run the country or the palace, but because you're the woman I want to share my life with. That I need to share my life with."

Emotion flickered across her lovely face and made hope spark inside him. "I do love you, Andi. I love you with all my heart and soul, with parts of me that I never knew existed. I tried to ignore the new tender feelings starting inside me because they scared me. It was easier to talk myself into using practical reasons to keep you. To convince myself I was still in full control of my emotions, that I didn't truly need you, or anyone else." He drew in a ragged breath. "But I do need you."

He paused, emotions streaming through his brain and

mind. How hard it was to put into words things that he could only understand at gut level. "I didn't know until now that I've been living a half life, devoid of emotion and even of true joy. In your arms I've found happiness I never knew existed."

He blinked, embarrassed by his frank confession. "I know you no longer believe me when I tell you I love you." He shook his head. "I don't blame you. Those words have lost their power. They've been used too many times. I don't know how to express what I truly feel except to say that my life is empty and hollow without you. Please don't leave me, Andi."

Andi blinked, eyelashes thick with tears. The raw emotion in his voice stunned her. He was always so calm, so controlled, so in charge of every situation. Right now she could sense that every word he said was true.

No guile, no charm, no winning ways—just a heartfelt plea that shook her to her core.

She hadn't dared to utter a single word until now, and when she opened her mouth, the painful truth emerged. "I love you, Jake. I've always loved you." Why hide anything now? "I've loved you almost since the first day I came to work for you. You're kind and fair and thoughtful, and tough and strong when you need to be. I've admired you every day and dreamed about you every night."

Putting her thoughts into words took effort, but it was a relief to finally get them off her chest. "So you see, when my memories—and the resulting inhibitions—were erased, I fell so easily into the kind of relationship I've always dreamed of. I'm sure it was frightening to know that someone you've worked so closely with for years had those kind of feelings."

She shivered slightly. "I didn't want you to ever find out.

That's one of the main reasons I wanted to leave. It was all wrong from the start."

"But it's not wrong." Jake kept his gaze fixed on hers. "I was wrong to take advantage of you, but we're meant to be together. I don't want a ceremonial wife *or* an assistant. I want someone who'll remind me I've never been up the mountain, and who'll take me there. I don't want someone who'll take good minutes on my life, I want someone to live it with me and make it fuller and richer than I ever imagined."

Unable to hold still any longer, Andi reached out to him and clasped his hands. He was still holding the ring, the pretty, simple diamond she'd liked, and the fact that he'd brought it touched her deeply. "I was already cursing myself for leaving you—and Ruthenia. I felt like I was leaving a big chunk of my heart behind." She hesitated and drew in a breath. "I don't want to leave you behind."

"Then don't. I'll come with you. Ruthenia can get along without me for a while." He rose from the floor and sat on the seat beside her. "We should visit your parents. It seems only right that I should ask them for your hand in marriage." A twinkle of humor brightened his eyes. "And maybe I'll have better luck with them."

He held up the ring between finger and thumb. "Though it would be nice to put this ring somewhere safe, like your finger, so it doesn't get lost while we're traveling."

The ring blurred as Andi's eyes filled with tears. She pulled off her gloves and held out her bare hands, which trembled. "I will marry you, Jake." Her voice cracked and a violent shudder rocked her as the cool metal slid over her finger. The act felt far more powerful and meaningful than the first time, when she didn't even know who she was. "I do want to spend the rest of my life with you."

Now that Jake had poured out his feelings, everything

felt different. She no longer had any doubt that he loved her as much as she loved him. Sun poured in through the large railcar window, and the world outside seemed bright with promise. "I love the idea of going to see my family. They'll be thrilled to meet you. If this train ever gets moving again, that is."

Jake grinned. "Let's see what we can do about that. But, first things first." He slid his arm around her back and pulled her close. Andi's eyes slid shut as their lips met and she kissed him with all the pent-up passion and emotion she'd planned to lock away for the rest of her life. Relief and joy flooded through her and her heart exploded with happiness at the feel of his strong arms around her. When they finally pulled apart, blinking in the sun, she had a strange sensation of her life starting afresh from this moment.

"I love you, Jake." At last she could say it out loud without a hint of embarrassment or doubt. She'd waited years for this moment and it was sweeter than she'd ever dreamed.

"Not as much as I love you." Jake's eyes sparkled.

"You're so competitive."

"So are you." He grinned. "One more reason why we're perfect for each other." Then he pulled out his phone. "Now, let's see if we can get this train moving."

Epilogue

"Of course you need an assistant." Jake leaned in and kissed Andi's neck.

Piles of envelopes and résumés covered her desk. The prospect of going through them seemed more than daunting. "But we already have a full staff. And three nannies."

"You need someone just for you." He eased his thumbs down her spine. "So you can come up with a crazy plan for the weekend, and put her to work making it happen while you and I go for a stroll on the mountain."

"That's too decadent."

"It's an important part of any monarch's job to be decadent."

Andi laughed. "Says who?"

"The paparazzi. They don't want to cover a bunch of dull worker bees."

"True." She giggled. "They did have fun taking those ridiculous shots of me sailing when I was eight months pregnant."

"See? You're helping people earn their livelihood. And what about the tourists? They want glamour and excitement, romance and majesty, not a queen who licks her own envelopes."

"I can think of better things to lick." She raised a brow.

"Now that you put it that way, I think I'll cancel this afternoon's meeting on foreign policy."

"Don't you dare." She shot him a fierce glare. "Just save your energy for later." She stroked a finger over his strong hand, where it rested on her desk.

"Have I ever run out of energy?" He growled the question in her ear.

"Never. Now I know where our son gets it from." Little Lucas was a tireless eighteen-month-old bundle of energy. They'd managed with just two nannies until he learned to walk; after that, three—plus Andi—were required to keep up with him.

A joyful shriek outside the door alerted her that his morning nap must be over. Jake dodged to the side as little Lucas barreled into the room, blond curls bouncing. "Mama, read me a story!"

"Of course, sweetie."

"See? You need an assistant so you have someone to read through all these résumés for you while you read Lucas a story." Jake chuckled.

"You're hired." She winked and gathered Lucas into her arms. "Lucas and I have an appointment with Thomas the Tank Engine."

"And James the Red Engine." Lucas's serious face reminded her so much of Jake's sometimes, despite the pudgy dimpled cheeks.

"This sounds like a very important meeting. Perhaps I should attend, too."

"Most definitely. Foreign policy can wait. Tell them

Ruthenia just wants to be friends with everyone." Andi swept Lucas up in her arms as she stood.

"A very sensible approach. We'll just have a big party with cupcakes and tell everyone to play nicely." Jake squeezed Lucas's little hand.

"Chocolate cupcakes, 'kay, Daddy?"

"Hmm. Not sure. We might have to put a committee together to discuss the finer details."

"How 'bout rainbow sprinkles?" Lucas's bright blue eyes stared at his dad.

"If rainbow sprinkles are involved I'll just have to issue an executive order."

Lucas clapped his chubby hands together.

Andi shrugged. "I do like to be surrounded by men who can make important decisions without a lot of fuss. Really takes the pressure off. Where's the book?"

Lucas pointed at his nanny Claire, who stood in the doorway with a stack of paperbacks and a freshly made snack on a plate.

"Let's head for the garden." Andi moved to the door. "Claire, can you call ahead and have some blankets spread on the lawn? And maybe bring out Lucas's trike and stick horse." She tickled under his chin and he giggled. Then she glanced up at Jake. "See? I am getting better at not doing everything myself."

"Your efforts are admirable. And much needed since you'll soon be in the third trimester and Lucas isn't getting lighter." He picked his son up and held him in his arms. Lucas clapped both chubby palms against his cheeks and laughed aloud. "What if his sister has as much energy as he does?"

"Then we'll need six nannies. If we keep having kids there will be zero unemployment in Ruthenia."

Lucas arched his back, signaling his desire to be free on

his fast-moving feet. Jake put him gently down and they both watched as Lucas tore off down the corridor with Claire running after him. "How do people manage a toddler without a nanny while they're pregnant?" Already she could get a little short of breath climbing stairs without carrying anyone.

"I don't know. I always had a nanny." He winked.

"It's amazingly easy to get used to being spoiled rotten. Where's my dish of peeled grapes?"

They both laughed. They knew they worked hard, for much longer hours than most people. Andi had come to enjoy the routine round of entertaining. It felt good to bring people into their home and make them feel welcome. As the host she took special pleasure in making sure everyone had a good time, quite different than when she simply had to make sure the events ran smoothly.

Her parents had fallen in love with both Ruthenia and Jake. With her father newly retired and her mom only working during the school year, they'd allowed Jake and Andi to give them a quaint house right in the town as a "vacation home," insisting they wanted to visit regularly without being on top of the couple.

Andi's sister and her husband flew in for the wedding, and their little daughter was a flower girl in the majestic old town church where they said their vows. They now also came to visit regularly, and the sound of little Lucy's childish laughter bouncing off the palace walls had urged Andi and Jake into parenthood.

Since Lucas was born the palace no longer felt like a place of business where people slept, but was fully a family home, where people also worked.

The difference was subtle, but transformative. Jake slid his arms around her waist. "Would you like me to carry you downstairs, Your Majesty?"

"That won't be necessary." She wriggled against him, enjoying the flash of heat that always sparked between them when they touched. "But you can kiss me."

His lips met hers and her eyes slid closed. She could always lose herself in his kiss. She'd dreamed of it so long and come so close to never tasting him again. Her fingers played over the muscle of his chest through his tailored shirt.

She pulled back, lips humming with desire. "Hold that thought. I have a story to read and you have to bring about peace in our time. I'll see you tonight."

"And every night." His soft glance was loaded with suggestion.

She glanced down at her hand, where the simple diamond ring she'd first chosen sparkled behind her engraved wedding band. A smile crept over her mouth. "For the rest of our lives."

* * * * *

COMING NEXT MONTH

Available July 12, 2011

#2095 CAUGHT IN THE BILLIONAIRE'S EMBRACE
Elizabeth Bevarly

#2096 ONE NIGHT, TWO HEIRS
Maureen Child
Texas Cattleman's Club: The Showdown

#2097 THE TYCOON'S TEMPORARY BABY
Emily McKay
Billionaires and Babies

#2098 A LONE STAR LOVE AFFAIR
Sara Orwig
Stetsons & CEOs

#2099 ONE MONTH WITH THE MAGNATE
Michelle Celmer
Black Gold Billionaires

#2100 FALLING FOR THE PRINCESS
Sandra Hyatt

You can find more information on upcoming
Harlequin® titles, free excerpts and more at
www.HarlequinInsideRomance.com.

HDCNM0611

USA TODAY *bestselling author B.J. Daniels*
takes you on a trip to Whitehorse, Montana,
and the Chisholm Cattle Company.

RUSTLED

Available July 2011 from Harlequin Intrigue.

As the dust settled, Dawson got his first good look at the rustler. A pair of big Montana sky-blue eyes glared up at him from a face framed by blond curls.

A woman rustler?

"You have to let me go," she hollered as the roar of the stampeding cattle died off in the distance.

"So you can finish stealing my cattle? I don't think so." Dawson jerked the woman to her feet.

She reached for the gun strapped to her hip hidden under her long barn jacket.

He grabbed the weapon before she could, his eyes narrowing as he assessed her. "How many others are there?" he demanded, grabbing a fistful of her jacket. "I think you'd better start talking before I tear into you."

She tried to fight him off, but he was on to her tricks and pinned her to the ground. He was suddenly aware of the soft curves beneath the jean jacket she wore under her coat.

"You have to listen to me." She ground out the words from between her gritted teeth. "You have to let me go. If you don't they will come back for me and they will kill you. There are too many of them for you to fight off alone. You won't stand a chance and I don't want your blood on my hands."

"I'm touched by your concern for me. Especially after you just tried to pull a gun on me."

"I wasn't going to shoot you."

Dawson hauled her to her feet and walked her the rest of the way to his horse. Reaching into his saddlebag, he pulled out a length of rope.

"You can't tie me up."

He pulled her hands behind her back and began to tie her wrists together.

"If you let me go, I can keep them from coming back," she said. "You have my word." She let out an unladylike curse. "I'm just trying to save your sorry neck."

"And I'm just going after my cattle."

"Don't you mean your boss's cattle?"

"Those cattle are mine."

"*You're* a Chisholm?"

"Dawson Chisholm. And you are…?"

"Everyone calls me Jinx."

He chuckled. "I can see why."

Bronco busting, falling in love…it's all in a day's work.
Look for the rest of their story in

RUSTLED

Available July 2011 from Harlequin Intrigue
wherever books are sold.

HIEXP0711R

THE NOTORIOUS
WOLFES

A powerful dynasty,
where secrets and scandal never sleep!

Eight siblings, blessed with wealth, but denied the one
thing they wanted—a father's love. Haunted by their
past and driven to succeed, the Wolfes scattered to the
far corners of the globe. It's said that even the blackest
of souls can be healed by the purest of love....

But can the dynasty rise again?

8 volumes to collect and treasure!

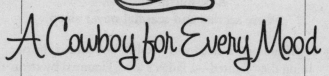